U0540176

漢英語法・語意學論集

陳重瑜著

臺灣 學生書局 印行

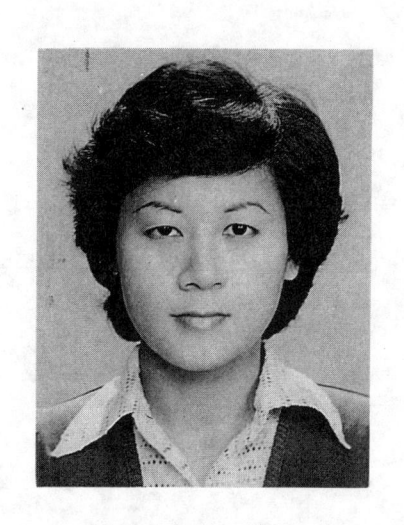

作者簡介：

陳重瑜；浙江鄞縣人，國立台灣大學外文系文學士，美國夏威夷大學語言學碩士，美國康奈爾大學語言學博士；曾任教于美國阿里桑那大學，新加坡南洋大學；現任新加坡國立大學華語研究中心高級研究員，并擔任教學工作。

「現代語言學論叢」緣起

　　語言與文字是人類歷史上最偉大的發明。有了語言，人類才能超越一切禽獸成為萬物之靈。有了文字，祖先的文化遺產才能綿延不絕，相傳到現在。尤有進者，人的思維或推理都以語言為媒介，因此如能揭開語言之謎，對於人心之探求至少就可以獲得一半的解答。

　　中國對於語文的研究有一段悠久而輝煌的歷史，成為漢學中最受人重視的一環。為了繼承這光榮的傳統並且繼續予以發揚光大起見，我們準備刊行「現代語言學論叢」。在這論叢裏，我們有系統地介紹並討論現代語言學的理論與方法，同時運用這些理論與方法，從事國語語音、語法、語意各方面的分析與研究。論叢將分為兩大類：甲類用國文撰寫，乙類用英文撰寫。我們希望將來還能開闢第三類，以容納國內研究所學生的論文。

　　在人文科學普遍遭受歧視的今天，「現代語言學論叢」的出版可以說是一個相當勇敢的嘗試。我們除了感謝臺北學生書局提供這難得的機會以外，還虔誠地呼籲國內外從事漢語語言學研究的學者不斷給予支持與鼓勵。

湯　廷　池

民國六十五年九月二十九日於臺北

語文教學叢書緣起

　　現代語言學是行為科學的一環,當行為科學在我國逐漸受到重視的時候,現代語言學卻還停留在拓荒的階段。

　　為了在中國推展這門嶄新的學科,我們幾年前成立了「現代語言學論叢編輯委員會」,計畫有系統地介紹現代語言學的理論與方法,並利用這些理論與方法從事國語與其他語言有關語音、語法、語意、語用等各方面的分析與研究。經過這幾年來的努力耕耘,總算出版了幾本尚足稱道的書,逐漸受到中外學者與一般讀者的重視。

　　今天是羣策羣力、和衷共濟的時代,少數幾個人究竟難成「氣候」。為了開展語言學的領域,我們決定在「現代語言學論叢」之外,編印「語文教學叢書」,專門出版討論中外語文教學理論與實際應用的著作。我們竭誠歡迎對現代語言學與語文教學懷有熱忱的朋友共同來開拓這塊「新生地」。

語文教學叢書編輯委員會　謹誌

湯　　序

　　在新加坡國立大學任教的陳重瑜博士是兼攻漢語語言學與英語語言學，並兼顧句法學與聲韻學的極少數語言學家之一。同時，陳博士是中央研究院歷史語言研究所主辦的第二屆國際漢學會議與美國康乃爾大學主辦的第三屆北美漢語語言學會議裡應邀發表論文的唯一女性語言學家。由此可見，陳博士在漢語語言學的研究上造詣之深與功力之高。令人遺憾的是，陳博士的論文一向都在國外的學術刊物上發表，國內的讀者也就較少拜讀的機會。因此，我們非常高興陳博士的新著《漢英語法・語意學論集》終於在國內順利出版。

　　《漢英語法・語意學論集》總共收錄論文八篇，其中五篇是關於漢語的，而三篇則是關於英語的。在有關漢語的論文中，第一篇論文〈動詞的動貌屬性與處所狀語的相對位置〉指出：出現於'他在玩呢'的'在'並不是由'他在那兒玩呢'裡刪略'那兒'得來的介詞，而是由'他在那兒在玩呢'裡經過介詞的'在'與動貌標誌的'在'之間的「疊音刪簡」（ haplology ）而得來的。第二篇論文〈漢語的動詞組補語〉根據內部結構的句法分析與多種方言的互相比較來證明：在'他走{得／的}快'裡引介補語'快'的助詞應該是'得'而不是'的'。而且，這個'得'之需要與否，主要取決於補語結構的語意類型。第三篇論文〈連謂結構「動詞'著'……動詞」的限制〉指出：「動詞。'著'……動詞」裡的兩個動詞並不表示兩個動作在同一時間發生,而在大多數情形下都表示一次只做一個動作。如果表示主事者主語同時做兩個動作，那麼就必須受到雙層語意限制：㈠這兩個動作彼此關連；㈡這兩個動作仍有主要與次要之分。這樣的分析可以說明爲什麼'他吃著飯說話'是病句。第四篇論文〈申論動詞詞尾'著'〉牽涉到作者與屈承熹先生之間有關「動詞'著'……動詞」結構的限制究竟是語意的抑或是語用的論爭。屈先生認爲這類連謂結構的限制是語用重於語意，而作者則認爲語意重於語用。第五篇論文〈關於'著'的答覆〉是作者針對「動詞'著'……動詞」結構的限制不可能是語意限制的反論，並指出以代換練習教學這個句型的缺失。

在有關英語的論文方面，第一篇論文〈英語動詞的時間結構〉主張：英語動詞的時間結構不應該把賓語或補語的存在考慮在內，因而不同意 Z. Vendler 有名的動詞分類。作者並主張：「持續性」與「非持續性」是英語動詞的時間結構唯一需要的區別。第二篇論文〈英語動詞的形體貌相〉指出：'sit, stand, put, hang'等動詞的形體貌相都含有「動態→靜態」的語意特徵；也就是「動態」的起動動作與「靜態」的後續狀態。以及物動詞爲例，「動態」的結束與「主事者」的消失導致「受事者」的自立，因而引起「及物→不及物」的演變。從「動態」到「靜態」，以及從「及物」到「不及物」的兩種變化，可以說明'He hung her picture on the cupboard'與'Her picture is hanging on the cupboard'這些例句間的語法與語意差異。第三篇論文〈英語狀態動詞的動性〉提議英語動詞的語意屬性應該區別「動性」(dynamic)與「動態」(active)，並且主張所有的英語動詞都是屬於「動性」的，然後在「動性」這個屬性下區別「動態」與「非動態」（即「靜態」）。作者認為這樣的分析可以說明含有「動性、非動態」屬性的狀態動詞可以出現於進行貌，而漢語的狀態動詞（俗稱形容詞）'漂亮、聰明、靜'等，眞正的「非動性」動詞則不能出現於進行貌。

以上八篇論文的內容一再顯現，語言分析中語法與語意的密不可分。因此，本書的英文書名就叫做 *Where Syntax and Semantics Fuse*（語法與語意的融合）。陳博士的語言分析一向嚴謹、細膩而富於創意，用字遣詞則簡鍊、扼要而順暢無碍。做為陳博士長年的同道，願意在此向國內的讀者鄭重推薦。

湯廷池

一九九二年三月八日

SOURCES

On Chinese:

1. Chen, Chung-yu. 1978. 'Aspectual Features of the Verb and the Relative Positions of the Locative'. Journal of Chinese Linguistics (U.S.A.) 6.1: 76-103.

2. Chen, Chung-yu. 1979. 'On Predicative Complements'. Journal of Chinese Linguistics (U.S.A.) 7.1: 44-64.

3. Chen, Chung-yu. 1986. 'Constraints on the 'V1-zhe...V2' Structure'. Journal of the Chinese Language Teachers Association (U.S.A.) 21.1: 1-20.

4. Chen, Chung-yu. 1987. 'Stemming from the Verbal Suffix -zhe'. Journal of the Chinese Language Teachers Association (U.S.A.) 22.1: 43-64.

5. Chen, Chung-yu. 1987. 'Reply to a Note on -zhe'. Journal of the Chinese Language Teachers Association (U.S.A.) 22.3: 67-72.

On English:

6. Chen, Chung-yu. 1982. 'Time Structure of English Verbs'. Papers in Linguistics (Canada) 15.3: 181-190.

7. Chen, Chung-yu. 1986. 'On the Physical Modality of English Verbs'. Papers in Linguistics (Canada) 19.2: 131-154.

8. Chen, Chung-yu. 'Dynamism in the English Stative Verbs'.

TABLE OF CONTENTS

「現代語言學論叢」緣起	I
湯　序	III
Sources	VII
A Sketch of the Papers	XI
1. Aspectual Features of the Verb and the Relative Positions of the Locative	1
2. On Predicative Complements	35
3. Constraints on the 'V1-zhe...V2' Structure	59
4. Stemming from the Verbal Suffix -zhe	79
5. Reply to a Note on -zhe	101
6. Time Structure of English Verbs	107
7. On the Physical Modality of English Verbs	119
8. Dynamism in the English Stative Verbs	141
Index	163

A SKETCH OF THE PAPERS

Paper 1:

Sentences like (1) '他在玩呢' had been analyzed as a shortened form of (2) '他在那兒玩呢' (Chao 1968:333, 772) and '在', a preposition in a locative. In this paper, '在' was for the first time recognized as an aspect marker in sentences like (1), and in sentences like (2), which is devoid of any auxiliary element or a verbal suffix, the product of a distant haplology of an aspect marker and a preposition in a locative phrase. Preverbal and postverbal locatives can be reduced to the same underlying structure provided semantic features of the verb are allowed to enter into the formulation of transformational rules. Both locatives modify verbs.

Paper 2:

Through evidence in the internal structure as well as cross-dialectal comparisons, it was proved that the de particle in predicative complements (e.g. '他走 de 快') ought to be 得 rather than 的. Chao's predicative complements, complements of extent, and resultatvie complements can ultimately be reduced to the same underlying structure. When the complement is a clause or a verb denoting a scalar notion, particle 得 occurs between the main verb and the complement (e.g., 他氣得不吃飯了，他氣得半死); when the complement is a verb denoting a categorical notion, no particle occurs in between (e.g., 他氣死了).

Paper 3:

Contrary to the common assumption or description that structure 'V1-zhe...V2' marks "two actions that occur simultaneously", it is proved here that the great majority of the sentences of this type involve only one active action at one time on the part of the subject. When the subject is the agent for two [+active] actions occurring at the same time, this structure is subject to a two-fold semantic constraint: (1) the two actions denoted are interrelated in certain ways; (2) One of the actions is the dominant and the other is the subordiante; this relative weighting is reflected in the fixed order of the two verbs.

Paper 4:

This paper contains certain points of disagreement between Chauncey C. Chu and me on the structure 'V1-zhe...V2'. Chu contends that the constraints I have proposed are "largely pragmatic rather than semantic". My reply is that pragmatic situations are variables that may change the aspectual character of the verbs or the interrelationship between the actions denoted and hence the eligibility of the verbs for entering into the said structure; but they are not the constraints. And to speak of a "pragmatic constraint" is to speak of a formulation of behavioral variables, which is an impossibility.

Paper 5:

This paper replies to a criticism questioning the validity of my proposed semantic constraints on the 'V1-zhe...V2' structure. It also points out a potential danger in substitution drills as a teaching method.

Paper 6:

Although attempts have been made to refine Vendler's frame work of English verbs, this paper argues that verbs should not be discussed in the context of superimposed qualifications (e.g. *to draw a circle*) or quantifications (e.g. *to run a mile*). The contrast in [± durative] is not only a necessary and sufficient distinction in the time structure of English verbs, but also the only distinction that can be made without adding superimpositions to the verb.

Paper 7:

A type of physical modality which can be characterized as [+ → − active] for action verbs was identified for the first time in this paper. Verbs such as *sit, stand, put, hang*, ect. contain in themselves both the [+active] inceptive motion and the subsequent [− active] static state of affairs. In the case of transitive verbs, with the termination of the active phase and hence the demise of the agent, the recipient acquires a 'derived autonomy' and the verb undergoes another transmutation, [+ → − transitive]. These two types of transmutation account for the differences between "*He hung her picture on the cupboard*" and "*Her picture is hanging on the cupboard*".

Paper 8:

This paper proposes that all English verbs are [+dynamic] in modality, which constitutes a drastic departure from the universally acknowledged distinction between STATES and DYNAMIC SITUATIONS. A distinction is made between 'dynamic' (potent or viable) and 'active' (motional). It is under the feature [+dynamic] that comes the division of [± active]. This dynamism explains the admissibility of the state verbs, which have a modality of [+dynamic, -active], into the progressive aspect. It also points out that the Chinese state verbs (or the 'adjectives' by the laymen and some grammarians) are perhaps the genuine non-dynamic verbs.

ASPECTUAL FEATURES OF THE VERB AND THE RELATIVE POSITIONS OF THE LOCATIVES

Abstract.

Preverbal and postverbal locatives can be reduced to the same underlying structure provided semantic features of the verb are allowed to enter into the formulation of transformational rules. Both locatives modify verbs. Immediately preceding a verb, zai is an imperfective aspect marker. In the absence of an aspectual suffix of the verb or any auxiliary element indicating futurity, zai in a preverbal locative is both an imperfective marker and a preposition in the place adverbial. Consequently, such a structure is compatible only with verbs denoting durative or repetitive, active actions. When a verb suffix or an auxiliary is present, zai in a preverbal locative is a pure preposition. A terminal aspect marker Zero, which triggers the postposition of the locative, is identified. A postverbal locative thus denotes the location of the static state of affairs at the termination of an abrupt action or instantaneous transition, or the termination of an inceptive motion which results in a static position of the actor (e.g. tang 'lie') or the mere presence of the recipient (e.g. gua 'hang').

0. Introduction.

This paper sets out to find the fundamental functional differences between preverbal and postverbal locatives in Mandarin Chinese. The syntactic behaviors of the verbs are discussed in the context of compatibilities with locatives containing the element zai. Studies on preverbal and postverbal locatives to date are inadequate in not being able to provide a criterion for eliminating ungrammatical sentences. Underlying this inadequacy is the failure to recognize a correlation between the aspectual features of the verb and the relative positions of the locative. For example, Tai's semantic principle, the most recent work, is still faced with a number of difficulties which are fundamental. A few examples are giver below.

Tai (1975) claims that a preverbal locative denotes the location of an action or a state of affairs. Such an interpretation exerts no legitimate restrictions on the occurrence of sentences such as (la) if one wants to express the location where the person's 'dying' took place.

(1a) *他在厨房里死。
He died in the kitchen.

On the other hand, it offers no effectual explanation as to the difference between (la) and (2a).

(2a) 他在厨房里哭。
He's crying in the kitchen.

Regarding postverbal locatives, Tai states explicitly that a postverbal locative specifies the location of the participant as a result of the action in which he has participated. (2b) is not acceptable because, as Tai says, it is rather bizarre to say that someone is affected by his own crying so that his location is changed from somewhere else to the kitchen. Following his explanation, (1b) is to be read as 'someone is affected by his own death so that his location is changed from somewhere else to the kitchen'.

(1b) 他死在厨房里。
(2b) *他哭在厨房里。

However, for a person to die at a particular place, he must be there first before he dies. It follows that there involves no change of location in

(1b) before and after death took place. Thus, change of the location of the participant affected is not a necessary condition. 1

It has been shown that Tai's principle, the most recent analysis of the locatives, still fails to capture the crucial difference between the pairs of sentences discussed above. It is claimed here that the crucial difference lies in the compatibilities of the verbs with a preverbal zai. This paper thus begins with a discussion of the identity of the preverbal zai.

1. Initial Identification of the Status of the Preverbal *Zai*.

Before studying the function of zai in a preverbal or postverbal locative, a scrutiny of zai in a simpler structure may render some insight into the identities of zai in different place adverbials.

---

1. When comparing pairs of sentences, Tai sometimes makes no discrimination with respect to the inclusion of verb suffix -zhe or -le, the particle le, or the presence of another verb, etc. For example, there is an element le in (ia) (Tai's 23) but not in (iia) (Tai's 24), which has been marked as ungrammatical. However, if we reverse the presence of le, (iib) will be acceptable and (ib) will be unacceptable.

    (ia) 他睡了兩天。
          He has been in bed for two days.

    (iia) *他在床上兩天。

    (ib) *他睡兩天。

    (iib) 他在床上兩天了。

Furthermore, Tai regards the zai in (iia) as a constituent of the place adverbial. I, on the other hand, consider the zai in (iia) and (iib) a verb, and the zai a constituent of the place adverbial in (iii), where a verb shui 'sleep' is present.

    (iii) 他睡在床上兩天了。

1.1. Zai in the structure zai + V.

(3a) 他在玩呢。
He's playing.

(4) 他在等人。
He's waiting for someone.

(5) 祖國在呼喚。
The fatherland is calling (for us).

(6) 天色在變了。
The sky is changing color (the sky is lowering).

(7) 地殼不斷地在變動。
The crust of the earth is constantly changing.

Chao (1968: 333, 772) analyzes zai in such constructions as a preposition with its object omitted and subsequently interprets (3a) as a shortened form of (3b).

(3b) 他在那兒玩呢。
He's there playing.

While it is easy to insert ner 'there' into (3a, 4) and perhaps even (5, 6, 7), an identification of the location is, however, hardly plausible with (5, 6, 7). Even if we could reconcile ourselves to the vague and, perhaps, semantically empty 'there', there still remain some syntactic difficulties: if zai is merely a preposition, why is it not possible to add a duration adverb to (3a) just as we can do with (3b), as shown in (3c, 3d)?

(3c) *他在玩了一整天了。

(3d) 他在那兒玩了一整天了。
He has been playing there for a whole day.

To supply another example, if a foreign student wants to express 'He's there dying', and follows the pattern in (3b), he will end up with (8a). And if he shortens it in this specific manner, he will obtain (8b).

  (8a) *他在那兒死。

  (8b) *他在死。
     He's there dying.

Nevertheless, neither of them is acceptable. What is wrong here? To this question neither Chao's interpretation of (3a) nor Tai's principle can offer an answer.

  Both pairs of counterexamples, (3c) and (3d), (8a) and (8b), point to the same direction: <u>Zai</u> in a preverbal position (when the verb contains no aspectual suffix) is not simply a preposition, and there is a certain connection between <u>zai</u> and the verb. For further elaboration of the argument that <u>zai</u> in sentences like (3b) is not merely a preposition and that (3a) is not necessarily a shortened form of (3b), we will try a simple test.

  (9a) 他在那兒哭 (睡/打電話)。
     He's there crying (sleeping/making a phone call).

  (9b) 他哭 (睡/打電話)。
  (9c) 他在哭 (睡/打電話)。

Ask any competent native speaker to subtract the information on the location, i.e. the locative, from (9a), and the resultant form will not be (9b), but (9c) where <u>zai</u> still remains. (9b) is incomplete with respect to temporal reference of the action. This is a positive indication that <u>zai</u> in (9a) is more than a mere preposition and that <u>zai</u> in (9c) is not a preposition with its object omitted. These examples also provide counter-evidence to the analysis of sentences like (9a) into two minor structures, S1 and S2, as represented by (9b) and (9d).

(9d)   他在那兒。
       He's there.

I shall explore the connection between zai and the verbs by listing and comparing some verbs which may occur immediately after zai without a place word in between, and those which may not occur in such a position. To avoid complications or confusion, at this stage I shall confine myself to intransitive action verbs (with or without cognate objects). Verbs denoting static positions (e.g. 躺 'lie', 坐 'sit', etc.) and transitive verbs will be discussed in later sections.

Type 1: intransitive verbs which may occur immediately after zai.:
哭 'cry', 爬 'crawl', 走 'walk', 飛 'fly', 唱歌 'sing', 跳舞 'dance', 游泳 'swim', 呼吸 'breathe', 生氣 'be angry' ...

(10a) 他在哭(唱歌)。
       He is crying (singing).

Type 2: intransitive verbs which may not occur immediately after zai:
  a: 跌 'fall/trip', 摔 'fall/trip', 倒 'collapse', 掉 'drop', ...

  b: 死 'die', 昏倒 'faint (and fall)', 醉倒 'get drunk (and fall)', 凍死 'freeze to death', 發生 'occur', 出現 'appear, emerge' ...

(11a) *他在跌(死/昏倒)。
       *He is tripping (being dead/fainting).

A comparison of Type 1 and Type 2 verbs reveals that all the verbs of Type 1 denote actions which are durable or repetitive, actions which occupy a relatively long span of time during the course of their occurrence, whereas verbs of Type 2 denote actions which take a very short time from inception to completion, or involve instantaneous change of status. I shall refer to verbs of Type 1 as durable action verbs, and those of Type 2 as abrupt action or instantaneous transition verbs (Cf. Section 3).

I may now draw two preliminary assumptions: 1) Zai immediately preceding a verb is not a preposition. 2) The fact that zai may precede only durable action verbs and may not precede abrupt action or instantaneous transition verbs clearly indicates that zai in such a position is a kind of aspect marker, marking a durable commitment, signaling that the actor is engaged in performing the action during a certain period of time or as a habitual activity.

The validity of this dichotomy of (intransitive) active action verbs can be verified by a comparison of a minimal pair, (12a) and (12b).

(12a) 他哭了很久了。(V.1)
He's been crying for a long time.

(12b) 他死了很久了。(V.2b)
It's been a long time since he died.

While the duration adverb in (12a) denotes the duration of the action, the duration adverb in (12b) denotes the lapse of time since the completion of the action. Moreover, the two superficially parallel constructions are indeed different structures. In (12a) the duration adverb modifies the verb; in (12b) the duration adverb modifies the whole preceding clause, and the sentence is a topic-comment construction. To sum up, verbs of Type 2, both subgroups b and a (e.g. 12c), are incapable of taking a duration adverb.

(12c) *他跌了很久了。(V.2a)
*He's been falling for a long time.

The compatibilities of duration adverbs with the two types of verbs suffice a positive confirmation of the dichotomy made in the present framework with respect to action types or verb types, which in turn testifies that zai immediately preceding a verb is an aspect marker.

1.2. Zai in the structure *Zai* + Place Word + V.

(10b)　他在客廳裡哭 (唱歌)。
　　　He's crying (singing) in the living room.

(11b)　*他在地上跌 (死/昏倒)。
　　　*He's tripping (dying, fainting) on the floor.

It is found that only verbs of Type 1, verbs which may occur in the pattern *zai* + V (hereafter Pattern O), may occur in the pattern *zai* + place word + V (hereafter Pattern A). Verbs of Type 2, which do not occur in Pattern O, do not occur in Pattern A either. Since it has been established that zai in Pattern O is an aspect marker, the situation is self-evident. *Zai* in Pattern A has a two-fold function: It is an aspect marker of the verb, marking an active on-going commitment, i.e., the actor is engaged in performing an action which is durable (thus entailing Type 1 verbs and precluding Type 2 verbs), as well as a preposition in the place adverbial. Put more explicitly, zai in a preverbal locative (when the verb contains no aspectual suffix) is virtually a haplology of the aspect marker of the verb and the preposition in the place adverbial. As the two forms are not linearly immediate to each other, we here speak of a case of distant haplology. The structure of (10b) is represented by (13a).

The operation involved in (13a) is phonologically a deletion and syntactically a haplology, because the preverbal zai does have government over the verb. This is precisely the theoretical basis of eliminating ungrammatical sentences such as (1a).

(13a, b):

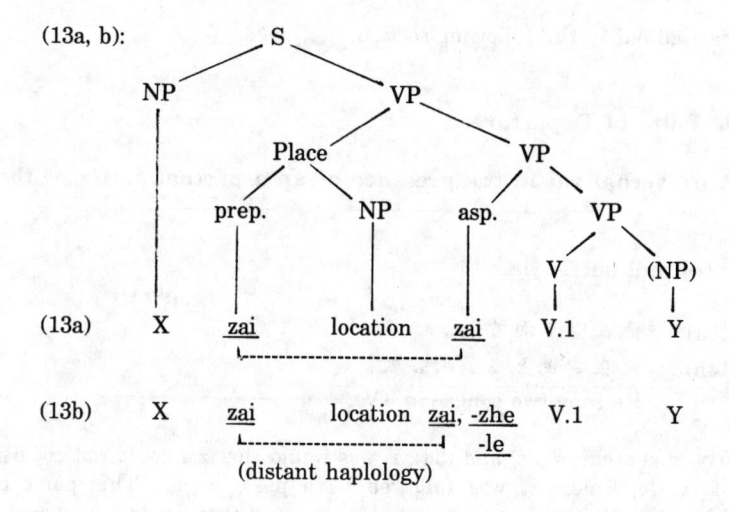

```
                    S
                 /     \
               NP       VP
                      /    \
                   Place    VP
                   /  \    /  \
                prep. NP  asp. VP
                                /  \
                               V   (NP)
```

(13a)   X   zai   location   zai   V.1   Y
               └─────────────────┘

(13b)   X   zai   location zai, -zhe   V.1   Y
               └─────────────┘   -le
               (distant haplology)

1.3. Zai in the structure V + zai + Place Word.

(10c) *他哭 (唱歌) 在客廳里。
(11c) 他跌 (死/昏倒) 在地上。

It is found that only Type 2 verbs, i.e. verbs of abrupt actions or instantaneous transitions, occur in the pattern V + zai + place word (hereafter Pattern B); Type 1 verbs do not occur in such a position. The function of postverbal locatives will be probed further in Section 2.2. Zai in a postverbal position is a pure preposition.

The correlation between verb types and the relative positions of the locative strongly suggests that pre- and postverbal locatives can be derived from the same underlying structure, one that contains a preverbal locative. In the absence of an aspectual suffix, Type 2 verbs, being incompatible with zai as an aspect marker, rush ahead to escape government of zai (Cf. Section 2.2). Further investigation on the reducibility of the two locatives will be carried out in the following section.

2. The Point of Departure.

2.1. A preverbal zai in the presence of an aspectual suffix of the verb.

2.1.1. Zai and suffix -le.

  (14a) *他在唱了兩首歌。
  (14b) 他在電視上唱了兩首歌。
      He sang two songs (on TV).

  Early in sentences (3c) and (3d), it was found that zai could not coexist with suffix -le, unless it was followed by a place word. This point is verified by (14a, b). As it has already been proved that zai in the absence of a verb suffix is an aspect marker, marking an on-going active commitment, the incompatibility between -le, which marks the completion of an action, and zai (as in (3c) and (14a)) needs no further explanation. When followed by a place word, a preverbal zai does cooccur with -le (as in (3d) and (14b)). In such cases, the preverbal zai is a pure preposition. The -le in (14c), where zai is not followed by a place word, is but a sentence particle, signaling a change of state.

  (14c) 他在唱了。
      Now he's singing.

2.1.2. Zai and suffix -zhe.

  Both zai as an aspect marker and -zhe, an aspectual suffix, signal the progress of an action. It is thus necessary to probe into the difference in their denotations of temporal contours as well as the relative distribution of the two.

(15a) 他在哭。
(15b) *他哭着。
He's crying.

(15c) 他還在哭。
(15d) *他還哭着。
He's still crying.

(15e) *他在哭說…。
(15f) 他哭着說…。
He said when crying ... .

(15g) 他在哭着。
(15h) 他在客廳里哭。
(15i) 他在客廳里哭着呢。
He's crying (in the living room).

The time references in (15a) vs (15f), together with the compatibilties with the time adverb hai 'still' ((15c) vs (15d)), indicate that the temporal contour marked by zai is wider in range and less precise than that marked by the suffix -zhe. Since the temporal denotations of the two markers are overlapping rather than contrasting, they may cooccur to express emphasis (15g).

Moreover, it seems that zai can be used for actions in actual progress as well as habitual activities, whereas -zhe is limited to actions in actual progress only. The contrasts between (16a) and (16b), (16e) and (16f) illustrate this point.

(16a) 他現在在路邊擺書攤(呢)。
He is now making a living by selling books by the roadside.

(16b) 他現在在路邊擺着書攤呢。
At this moment he is attending to his book stand by the roadside.

(16c) 他在上課。
(16d) 他上着課(呢)。
He's in class now.

(16e) 他在上大學。
(16f) *他上着大學。
He's at the university.

Now I am able to make a distinction between the two markers denoting progress: Zai is an imperfective marker, which can be used for either actions in actual progress or habitual activities; zhe is a progressive marker, which seems to be limited to actions in actual progress only. The temporal contour marked by zai is wider in range thus less precise than that marked by -zhe.

To sum up, in the absence of an aspectual suffix of the verb, zai in a preverbal locative is both an imperfective marker of the verb and a preposition in the place adverbial. When verb suffix -le is present, a preverbal zai is a pure preposition. In the presence of suffix -zhe, zai is a pure preposition when followed by a place word. Without a following place word, zai may still cooccur with -zhe to express emphasis. Structure (13a) can now be revised to (13b). Aimed at a simple and lucid presentation, structures (13) and (22) (in later discussion) represent basic structures only. The utilization of both the imperfective marker and the progressive maker in sentences such as (15g) is an emphatic device. The distribution of the three aspect markers can be formulated as follows: (zai ∮ -zhe), le.

Distant haplology refers to the merging of the preposition zai with the aspect marker zai of the main verb of the sentence.

(17a) 他在家里看書。(--distant haplology)
He is studying at home.

(17b) 他喜歡在家里看書。(--no haplology involved)
He likes to study at home.

The <u>zai</u> in sentence (17a), for example, is a product of haplology and has a dual function; the <u>zai</u> in (17b), on the other hand, is a pure preposition. In (17b), <u>xihuan</u> is the main verb; <u>zai jia-li kan shu</u> is the object of the main verb. As <u>kanshu</u> is not the main verb of the sentence (it is a verb phrase, unmarked as to aspect, which is comparable to an infinitive in English), the <u>zai</u>, which occurs after the main verb, cannot be an aspect marker but a pure preposition.

Moreover, in sentences such as (18a, b, c), which contain either an imperative marker or an auxiliary element to indicate futurity, the preverbal <u>zai</u> is also a pure preposition.

(18a) 在我家吃頓飯吧。
Why don't you (stay and) have dinner with us.

(18b) 你在客廳里睡一覺吧。
Well, take a nap in the living room then.

(18c) 可別在樓梯上跌一交。
Be sure not to have a fall on the stairs.

2.2. Postverbal locatives and the terminal aspect marker.

(1b) 他死在厨房里。

(19) 一顆椰子掉在屋頂上。
A coconut fell on the roof.

(20a) 他跌在樓梯上。
He fell on the stairs.

(20b) 他在樓梯上跌了一交。
He had a fall on the stairs.

(20c) *他在樓梯上跌一交。
(20d) *他跌了一交在樓梯上。

It is found that when an intransitive verb of Type 2 is followed by a cognate object, which in these sentences functions as measure for the verb (Cf. Chao 1968:585), it occurs with a preverbal locative (20b, as opposed to 20d). Sentences (1b, 19, 20a) which do not possess a cognate objects, contain a postverbal locative. Sentence (20c), which contains a preverbal <u>zai</u> and a verb of Type 2 in the absence of an auxiliary or verbal suffix is incomplete as to aspect markers. With this initial observation, I render sentences (1b, 19, 20a) into structure (21a) and sentence (20b) into (21b).

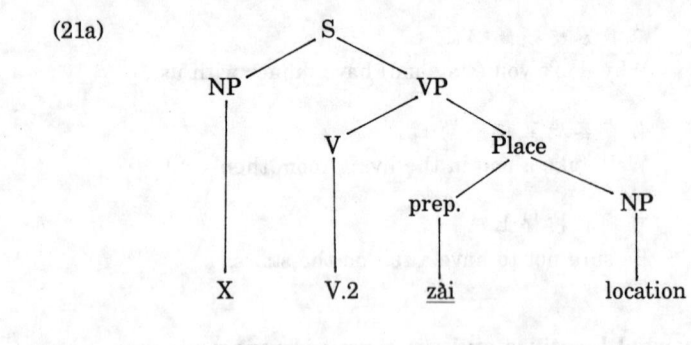

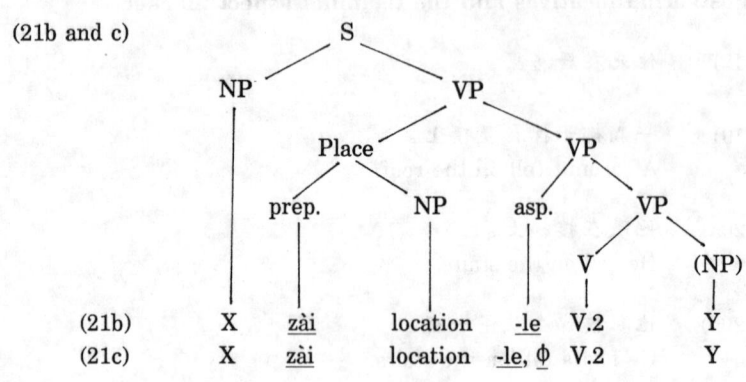

(21a)

```
            S
         /     \
        NP      VP
        |      /   \
        |     V     Place
        |     |    /    \
        |     |  prep.   NP
        |     |   |      |
        X    V.2  zài   location
```

(21b and c)

```
              S
           /     \
          NP      VP
          |      /   \
          |   Place   VP
          |   /  \   /  \
          | prep. NP asp. VP
          |  |   |   |   /  \
          |  |   |   |  V   (NP)
          |  |   |   |  |    |
(21b)     X zài location -le V.2  Y
(21c)     X zài location -le,φ V.2 Y
```

A question immediately arises when we compare (21a) with (21b); that is, why is there not an aspect marker in (21a)? Going through (1b, 19, 20a) again one is assured that although the perfective suffix -le is absent, the actions have already taken place. What, then, are the differences between the pair (20a) and (20b)? After a closer look, one finds that (20b), which contains a suffix -le, relates an action totally finished. It tells of a completed action. On the other hand, upon hearing sentence (20a), which does not contain a -le, one visualizes the person as lying or sitting on the stairs. In other words, the person has not yet got over with the fall. It is of paramount importance that this visual image is static. Sentence (20a), therefore, depicts a scene; the narration is tantamount to a snapshot or a quick-freeze of the state of affairs at the termination of the action, i.e. the instant of touch-down. The time reference marked by -le is indeed post-terminal. A distinction can thus be made between a perfective marker -le and a terminal marker ϕ, Zero.

To sum up, there is an aspect marker Zero which is compatible only with verbs of Type 2 but not with verbs of Type 1. When the aspect marker Zero occurs with a Type 2 verb, it designates a static state of affairs at the instant of touch-down, i.e. the terminal cross-section of the action. In fact, as denoting abrupt actions or instantaneous transitions, verbs of Type 2 really need not rely on suffix -le to indicate completion or termination; once these actions take place, they end almost instantly. This explains the incompatibility between aspect marker Zero and Type 1 verbs. As denoting durable actions, Type 1 verbs need the perfective suffix -le to signal completion, or else the action could go on and on.

The terminal marker, Zero, designates the terminal cross-section of an action which is [+active] and [-durable], with verbs which are [-active], [+durable] (i.e. verbs of static positions or presence, such as zuo 'sit', gua 'be hung'), marker Zero designates the termination of the active inceptive motion, which turns out to be an inactive, durable process. Consequently, the Zero marker denotes any cross-section of that process (Cf. Section 4).

As stated earlier, when a cognate object functioning as a measure for a verb is present, suffix -le must be selected (20b vs c). This rule also has its root in semantics; one cannot define the extent or magnitude of an action until it finishes completely. An assurance from the perfective suffix -le is, therefore, indispensable.

Having established a terminal aspect marker Zero, I am able to combine (21a) with (21b) and obtain (21c).

When Zero is selected for the aspect marker node, (21c) will yield a preverbal locative which appears like one derived from (15a) (i.e. *ta zai louti-shang die). However, the preverbal zai in products of (15a) is a haplology of an imperfective aspect marker and a preposition. As Type 2 verbs are incompatible with the imperfective marker zai, it is necessary to keep the verb out of the reach of zai. An obligatory transformation to permute the locative to a postverbal position is thus necessitated when the aspect node (together with the object node) in (21c) is represented by Zero. This is precisely the point of departure for the two locatives, which is deduced from a purely synchronic analysis.

The assumption of the underlying order for the zai locatives is a simplicity measure. The postulation of the preverbal position as the underlying order for zai locatives is justified on the basis of distribution, among the four aspect markers (the imperfective zai, the progressive -zhe, the perfective -le, and the terminal Zero), only the terminal marker occurs with a postverbal locative; the others occur with preverbal locatives.

Now structure (21c) turns out to be identical with (15b), which generates only preverbal locatives; only that owing to the nature of Type 2 verbs, the progressive marker -zhe and the imperfective marker zai never come up to represent the aspect node in (21c). On the other hand, marker Zero, being incompatible with Type 1 verbs, will never be selected for the aspect node in (15b). Having clarified the relationships between the verbs and various aspect markers, we can now reduce (15b) and (21c) to the same structure, (22).

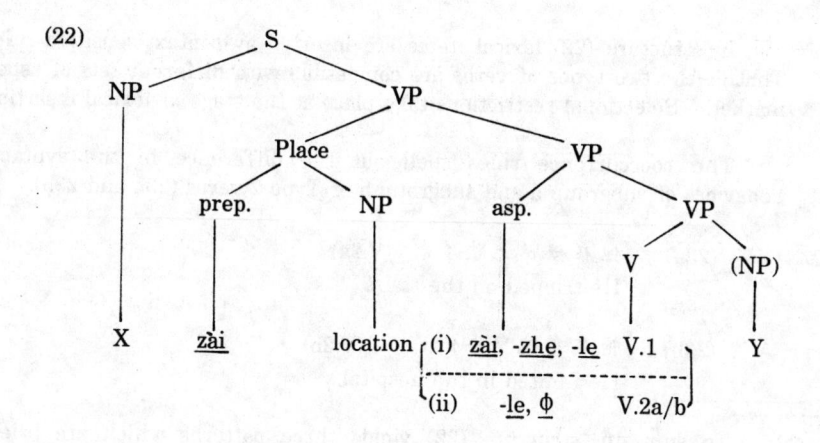

(22)
```
                    S
         ┌──────────┴──────────┐
        NP                     VP
         │          ┌──────────┴──────────┐
         │        Place                   VP
         │    ┌─────┴─────┐        ┌──────┴──────┐
         │   prep.        NP      asp.           VP
         │    │           │        │         ┌───┴───┐
         │    │           │        │         V      (NP)
         X   zài      location  (i) zài, -zhe, -le  V.1   Y
                                (ii) -le, ɸ        V.2a/b
```

Subcategorization rules:
  V.1   ([-transitive], [+active], [+durable])
  V.2a ([-transitive], [+active], [-durable],
         [-transition])
  V.2b ([-transitive], [+active], [-durable],
         [+transition])
  Y   [-concrete] (i.e. cognate object)

Cooccurrence rules:
  Y and -le, mutually dependent/ V. 2a
  Y requires -le/ V.2b

Transformational rules:
  SD: zai, location, zai, V.1   SC: 1,2,4
  SD: zai, location, ɸ, V.2a/b   SC: 3,4,1,2

Affix rule:
  SD: -zhe/-le, V(1, 2a/b)   SC: 2,1
  SD: ɸ, V. 2a/b   SC: 2,1

In structure (22) lexical items are inserted by context-sensitive rules. That is, the two types of verbs are compatible with different sets of aspect markers. Selectional restrictions take place at the stage of lexical insertion.

The cooccurrence rules spell out the difference in the syntactic behaviors of subgroup a and subgroup b of Type 2 verbs (23a and 23b).

(23a) *他在樓梯上跌了。 (V.2a)
       He tripped on the stairs.

(23b) 他在醫院里昏倒了。 (V.2b)
       He fainted in the hospital.

To sum up, structure (22) yields three patterns which are briefly annotated as follows:

Pattern S: Suffix -zhe or -le is present; zai is a pure preposition; the locative precedes the verb.
Pattern A: No verb suffix; zai is an imperfective marker as well as a preposition in the locative which precedes the verb.
Pattern B: No verb suffix; the terminal marker Zero is present; the locative follows the verb.

3. The Notion of Lexical Items and the Different Phases of an Action.

It has been shown in the previous section that preverbal and postverbal locatives can be reduced to the same underlying structure provided that semantic features of the verb are allowed to enter into the formulation of transformational rules. It is important to note that we are working on the basis of features rather than the verb itself; for a verb may denote different 'forms' of actions, and an action can be viewed in part or in whole.

The verb tiao 'leap, jump', for example, when referring to a series of repetitive actions acquires the feature [+durable] and thus occurs in Pattern A (24a; Tai 1975: (9a)). When referring to a single leap from one point to another, it denotes an abrupt action and possesses the feature [-durable], hence, occurs in Pattern B (24b; Tai 1975: (9b)).

(24a) 小猴子在馬背上跳。 (Pattern A)
The little monkey was jumping on the horse's back.

(24b) 小猴子跳在馬背上。 (Pattern B)
The little monkey jumped on the horse.

The verb tiao 'jump' as in (24a, b) is regarded as accommodating two lexical items. Here we follow the Weinreich-McCawley definition of lexical items (McCawley 1968). McCawley points out that the sentence *This coat is warm* is ambiguous between the meaning that the coat has a relatively high temperature and the meaning that it makes the wearer feel warm. He then proposes that English has two lexical items *warm*.

Some actions may have more than one aspectual phase. When the whole course of an action is being viewed, the verb denotes a durable process and occurs in Pattern A (25a; Tai 1975: (3b)). When the instant of touch-down, or the terminal cross-section of the action, is being focused on, the verb denotes an abrupt action and occurs in Pattern B (25b).

(25a) 黃梅細雨在窗外下個不停。(V.1-.P.A)
The early summer rain has been drizzling ceaselessly out there.

(25b) 雨下在地上。(V.2-P.B)
The rain fell on the ground.

Such susceptibilities of different readings or different aspectual phases are, possibly, confined to verbs possessing the feature [+venue] (i.e. venue-oriented or physical contact involved). The fact that certain verbs are capable of different readings and certain actions can be viewed in whole or in part indicates that an approach to the problems of preverbal versus postverbal locatives with verbs as minimal entities would be futile. The working parameters must be the aspectual features of the actual action which the verb denotes.

4. Verbs Denoting Static Positions or Presence.

4.1. Verbs denoting static positions.

Verbs such as tang 'lie', zuo 'sit', zhan 'stand', dun 'squat', gui 'kneel', etc. possess the features [-active], [+durable]. Although for every occurrence of such static postures, there has been a [+active] inception or onset, and the static portion is really the second phase of the action, the active inception is, nevertheless, not contained in the verb itself. To express the inceptive motion, a movement adverbial such as qilai 'up' or xiaqu 'down' is indispensable. Therefore, these verbs are marked [-active].

As stated earlier, the imperfective marker, zai, marks an active commitment. Verbs of static positions, being inactive, i.e., during the course of their occurrence the actor is not actively engaged in performing an action as such, do not occur with this marker zai. Hence, zai in (26a) can only be a pure preposition. Thus, (26a) is incomplete as to aspect reference.

(26a) *他在樹下坐 (躺)。 (P.A)
*He sits (/lies) under the tree.

(26b) 他在樹下坐着 (躺着)。 (P.S)
He's sitting (/lying) under the tree.

(26c) *他在樹下坐了 (躺了)。 (P.S)
(26d) 他在樹下坐了 (躺了) 十分鐘。 (P.S)
He sat (/lay) under the tree (for ten minutes).

(26e) 他坐 (躺) 在樹下。 (P.B)
He sat (/lay) under the tree.

These verbs may not occur with the perfective marker -le without a duration adverb to specify the temporal distribution (26c vs. d). They occur with the progressive marker -zhe and the terminal marker Zero (26b and e). Marker Zero indeed denotes the termination of the active inception, which (i.e. the termination) in this case is a durable static continuum. Consequently, the terminal aspect marker designates any cross-section of this continuum. Sentence (26e), for example, may denote the state of affairs at any moment within the ten minutes of (26d). For the sake of convenience, we shall refer to verbs of static positions as verbs of Type 3.²

4.2. Verbs denoting static presence.

  (27a) 我的車停在草地上。 (P.B)
     My car is parked on the lawn.

---

2. <u>Xiuxi</u> 'rest' is classified as a verb of static position by Chao (1968:671). However, its syntactic behavior indicates that it is a verb of durable actions, i.e. Type 1, in the present framework. (We are not comparing the two classifications as they aim at different things.) In fact, when a person is 'resting', he is not necessarily assuming a static position and doing nothing more. 'Rest' simply means to be away from the activity one is engaged in; yet while doing so one is still engaged in other activities (e.g. ii, iii).

  (1a) 他在樹下休息。(P.A.)
  (1b) *他休息在樹下。(P.B.)
     He's resting under the tree.

  (ii) 你睡了那麼久，休息够了吧？
     You've slept for such a long time, I suppose you've had enough rest.

  (iii) 別做了，休息一下，看場電影去吧。
     Stop working. Go to a movie and relax.

Another verb also meaning 'rest', <u>xie</u>, needs further investigation.

(27b)　他的衣服丢在地上。(P.B)
His clothes are left on the floor.

(27c)　那幅畫在客廳里掛着呢。(P.S)
That painting is hanging in the living room.

Although the verbs in (27a-c) are all different, the roles played by the subjects are the same; they are merely being present at a particular place. In other words, the different verbs in these sentences all denote the same thing; mere presence, which is static. This static presence is really a resultant phase of an active action. Such verbs are all [+venue], i.e. venue-oriented verbs. And in (27a-c), they share the feature [-transitive] and [-active]. Such a reading of the verbs in a recipient-result (hereafter R-R) construction has already deviated from the readings of these verbs in an actor-action (hereafter A-A) construction (which denotes the active inception). Therefore, I shall treat these verbs as accommodating two lexical items. For the sake of convenience, verbs such as those in (27a-c) are labelled verbs of Type 4.

As in the case of Type 3 verbs, the feature [-active] readily prescribes incompatibilities with the imperfective marker zai (28a) and the perfective suffix -le in the absence of a duration adverb (28b vs c).

(28a)　*那幅畫在這里掛。(P.A)
That painting is hanging here.

(28b)　*那幅畫在這里掛了。(P.S)
(28c)　那幅畫在這里掛了兩天了。(P.S)
That painting has been hanging here (for two days).

I shall discuss Type 4 verbs in terms of their compatibilities with aspect markers -zhe and Zero.

(29)　Frame 1: NP zai neili V-zhe. (Pattern S)
　　　Frame 2: NP V zai neili. (Pattern E)

Filler sets:

(a)	那幅畫	'that painting'	掛	'hang'
(b)	你的書	'your book'	放	'put'
(c)	他的車	'his car'	停	'park'
(d)	他的衣服	'his clothes'	丟	'throw'
(e)	他的名字	'his name'	寫	'write'
(f)	玫瑰花	'the roses'	種	'plant'

Frames 1 and 2 in (29) constitute a simple device to detect differences in the syntatic behaviors of Type 4 verbs. It is found that filler sets a-c can fill both frames, whereas sets d-f can fill only Frame 2. Thus, a distinction is made between Type 4a, verbs such as those in sets a-c, and Type 4b, verbs such as those in d-f.

While sentences derived from Frame 2 depict dead consequential phenomena, sentences derived from Frame 1 account for on-going existence (as marked by the progressive marker -zhe). This is where verbs of Type 4a and those of Type 4b diverge. This difference can be further attributed to the feature [durable]: verbs of Type 4a are [+durable] (when they are read as [-transitive] and [-active], hence, they may denote either a static continuum (in Frame 1) or a dead consequential state or phenomenon (in Frame 2), which is a cross-section of the static continuum. We can speak of 'derived autonomy' for the inanimate subjects in sentences derived from Frame 1. (Chafe (1970) speaks of 'derived potency' for inanimate nouns playing an agentive role in sentences containing an active verb. As Type 4 verbs are [-active], it should suffice to speak of 'derived autonomy' for the subjects in sentences derived from Frame 1.) Type 4b verbs, on the other hand, are [-durable] (in the context of [-transitive] and [-active]), and thus only occur in Frame 2, denoting a dead consequential phenomenon.

The syntactic behaviors of verbs of Type 3 and Type 4 are outlined in (30), which is basically the same structure as (22). The affix rule and transformational rules are not repeated in (30).

(30)

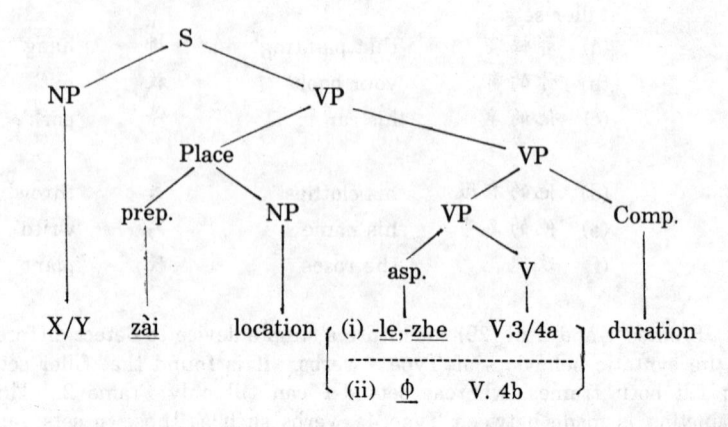

```
                    S
         ┌──────────┴──────────┐
        NP                     VP
         │          ┌──────────┴──────────┐
         │        Place                   VP
         │     ┌────┴────┐        ┌───────┴───────┐
         │   prep.      NP        VP            Comp.
         │     │        │       ┌─┴─┐             │
         │     │        │     asp.  V             │
         │     │        │       │   │             │
        X/Y   zài    location (i) -le,-zhe   V.3/4a   duration
                             ------------------------
                             (ii)   φ      V. 4b
```

Subcategorization rules:
V.3   ([-transitive], [-active], [+durable])
V.4a   ([-transitive], [-active], [+durable])
V.4b   ([-transitive], [-active], [-durable])
X   [+animate]
Y   [-animate]

Cooccurrence rules:
1. -le, duration: mutually dependent
2. -zhe/φ , duration: mutually exclusive
3. X occurs with V.3
4. Y occurs with V.4a/b

Table (31) is a summary of the aspectual features and syntactic behaviors of the intransitive verbs dealt with so far.

(31)

Denotation of the verb:

Type 1: durable or repetitive action
    2: a: abrupt action
       b: instantaneous transition
    3: static position
    4: static presence
       a: persistent existence or dead phenomenon
       b: dead phenomenon

Verb Type	1	2 a	2 b	3	4 a	4 b
Features:						
[durable]	+	−	−	+	+	−
[active]	+	+	+	−	−	−
[transition]		−	+			
Compatibilities with patterns:						
(P.A) zai	+	−	−	−	−	−
(P.B) ϕ	−	+	+	+	+	+
(P.S) -zhe	+	−	−	+	+	−
(P.S) -le	+	−	+	−	−	−
(P.S) -le + comp*	+	+	+	+	+	−
Functional structure of the sentence	actor-action				recipient-result	

* Comp: complement: duration adverb or cognate object.

(32a) 他在客廳里睡(等)。 (P.A)
(32b) 他睡(等)在客廳里。 (P.B)
He's sleeping (waiting) in the living room.

(33a) 他在上海住。 (P.A)
(33b) 他住在上海。 (P.B)
He lives in Shanghai.

Verbs such as shui 'sleep', deng 'wait', zhu 'live', have the feature [+durable]. Whether these actions are [+active] or [-active] is, nevertheless, a very controversial question. This quasi-active nature of the verbs is, perhaps, the crucial feature which enables them to enter into both patterns. It is also possible that there are other features not yet discovered, which are responsible for this peculiar syntactic behavior.

Li and Thompson (1974) regard (33a) and (33b) as paraphrases and conclude that the preverbal zai in (33a) is a preposition just like the postverbal zai in (33b). In fact, this happens to be a case where idiosyncratic features of the verb have come in and obscured the correlation between the features of the verb and its compatibilities with the two patterns.

6. Transitive Verbs.

The binary distinction within active intransitive verbs (i.e. Type 1, [+durable]; Type 2, [-durable]) also exists in active transitive verbs. The transitive verbs share all the syntactic behaviors with their intransitive counterparts. Type 1 and Type 2 may now be expanded to include transitive verbs.

Type 1: xie 'write', kan 'read, see', zhao 'look for', mai 'buy', kaolü 'consider', jihua 'plan' ...
Type 2: diao 'lose', diu 'throw, lose', shuai 'throw', faxian 'discover', faming 'invent' ...

The difference between subgroups a and b for intransitive Type 2 verbs, which pertains to the compatibility with suffix -le in the absence of a cognate object, neutralizes in the case of transitive verbs; as an object is always present or implicit in the sentence.

As stated in Section 4.2, venue-oriented [+transitive] and [+active] verbs may evolve into [-transitive] and [-active] ones (i.e. verbs of Type 4) after the resultant static phase (34b, 35b) splits off from the active inception. An account of both the active action (34a, 35a) and the resultant state prior to a complete split-off (i.e. the simultaneous state of affairs at the moment of touch-down) gives rise to sentences such as (34c, 35c).

(34a)　他在馬路上丟了一張糖紙。　(P.S)
　　　　On the road he threw away a piece of candy wrap.

(34b)　一張糖紙丟在地上。　(P.B)
　　　　A piece of candy wrap has been thrown on the ground.

(34c)　他在馬路上丟了一張糖紙在地上。
　　　　On the road he threw a piece of candy wrap on the ground.

(35a)　他在樓下掛了一幅畫。　(P.S)
　　　　He hung a picture downstairs.

(35b)　一幅畫掛在牆上。　(P.B)
　　　　A picture has been hung on the wall. (Cf. 27c)

(35c)　他在樓下掛了一幅畫在牆上。
　　　　He hung a picture on the wall downstairs.[3]

(36a) represents the structure underlying (34c) and (35c). As the

---

3. Sentences (35a. c) and (35d) in later discussion correspond respectively to Tai's v, vi, vii in his footnote 12, which puzzled him. Structure 36a with its surface manifestations 36b-d should be able to clarity the confusion involved.

structure is indeed a fusion of an action and a state, I shall refer to (36a) as Structure F. Transformational rules and aspectual markers, which by now are predictable, are not specified there (Cf. 22 and 30).

(36a)

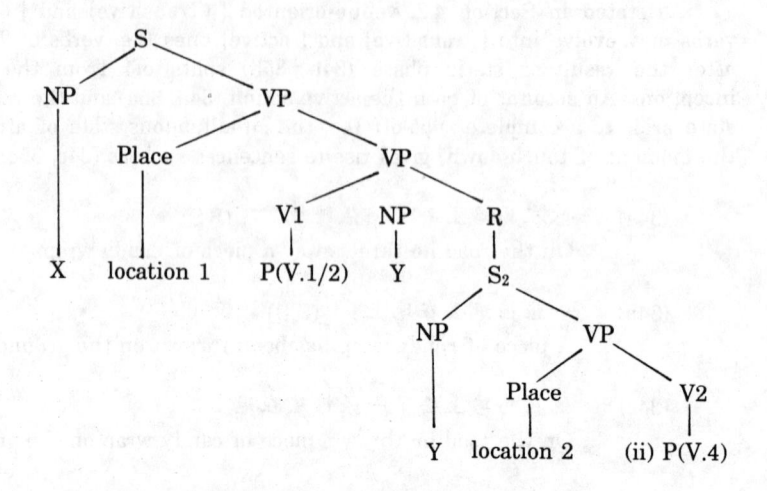

```
                    S
                   / \
                 NP   VP
                 |   / \
                 |  Place VP
                 |   |   / \
                 |   |  V1  NP  R
                 |   |  |   |   |
                 X location1 P(V.1/2) Y  S₂
                                        / \
                                       NP  VP
                                       |  /  \
                                       | Place V2
                                       |  |    |
                                       Y location2 (ii) P(V.4)
```

> Subcategorization rules:
> P: V1 and V2 are phonologically identical.
>   V.1/2 ([+venue], [+transitive], [+active])
>   V.4 ([+venue], [-transitive], [-active])

In structure (36a), R denotes the simultaneous resultant state of affairs of S1 (which is S minus S2). The Type 4 verb in S2 thus denotes a dead consequential phenomenon rather than a persistent existence of Y, as indicated by aspect marker set (ii) (Cf. 30). It follows that S2 yields a structure wherein locative 2 occurs after V2. Locative 1 always precedes V1. S1 is the structure underlying (34a) and (35a); S2 is the structure underlying (34b) and (35b). After the deletion of phonologically identical items, (36a) yields a surface structure of Pattern F1 (36b), as manifested in (34c) and (35c).

(36b)　　X + locative 1 + V + Y + locative 2　(P.F1)

In pattern F1, locative 1 modifies the verb, or the action. Locative 2, which appears to modify Y, in fact modifies V2 in the deep structure, which denotes the location of the presence of Y and is deleted in the surface structure.

The restriction that V1 and V2 share the same phonological shape, or better put, that only verbs capable of transmutations of the forms {+→ -transitive} and {+→ -active} are able to trigger such a fusion of structures, has important implications. It is a powerful constraint for eliminating ungrammatical sentences such as (37) and (38), wherein the verbs are not capable of such transmutations.

(37)　　*他炒菜在鍋里。
　　　　He cooked some vegetables in the pan.

(38)　　*他買書在書店里。
　　　　He bought some books at the bookstore.

Structure (36a) yields a surface structure of Pattern F2 (36c) as illustrated by (34d) and (35d), when locative 1 is not expressed.

(36c)　　X + V + Y + locative 2　(P.F2)
(34d)　　他丟了一張糖紙在地上。(P.F2)
(35d)　　他掛了一幅畫在牆上。(P.F2)

In case the object is already understood, Y is omitted and Pattern F1 is further shortened to Pattern F3 (36d) as illustrated by (34e) and (35e).

(36d)　　X + V + locative 2　(P.F3)
(34e)　　他丟 (了) 在地上。(P.F3)
(35e)　　他掛 (了) 在牆上。(P.F3)

A few more examples of Patterns F1-3 are given in (39a, b) and (40).

(39a)　他（在教室里）寫了幾個字在黑板上。　(P.F1, P.F2)
(39b)　他寫（了）在黑板上。　(P.F3)
　　　　(In the classroom) he wrote (a few characters) on the blackboard.

(40)　　你放（了）在那里嗎？ (P. F3)
　　　　Did you put it there?

7. Place Adverbials in <u>Ba</u> Constructions.

In the discussion on <u>ba</u> constructions, I am concerned only with those which contain a place adverbial in a post-<u>ba</u> position.

With verbs capable of transmutations in the forms of {+ → -transitive} and {+ → -active}, the post-<u>ba</u> locative follows the verb (41b and 42b). In such cases the actual action (rather than the abstract 'disposal') finishes at, or prior to, the moment the recipient lands on the location. The post-<u>ba</u> postverbal locative then modifies a static state of affairs at the termination of the action.

(41a)　　*他把刀在水池里丟。
(41b)　　他把刀丟在水池里。
　　　　　He threw the knife into the pond.

(42a)　　*他在教室里把答案在黑板上寫。
(42b)　　他在教室里把答案寫在黑板上。
　　　　　In the classroom he wrote the answers on the blackboard.

With verbs incapable of the above-mentioned transmutations, the post-<u>ba</u> locative precedes the verb (43a and 44a). And in such cases, the actual action continues after the initial landing of the recipient on the location. A post-<u>ba</u> preverbal locative modifies a durable action.

(43a)　他把刀在石頭上磨。
(43b)　*他把刀磨在石頭上。
　　　　He sharpened the knife on a stone.

(44a)　別把手帕在我面前揚來揚去。
(44b)　*別把手帕揚來揚去在我面前。
　　　　Stop waving your handkerchief in front of me.

8. Closing Words.

The correlation between the aspectual features of the verb and the relative positions of the locative in a sentence is verified again in ba constructions. This correlation, however, applies only to action verbs and pragmatic situations. It cannot apply to idiomatic metaphorical speech where the action is not meant to be materialized (45).

(45)　我看在你父親的面上.... (V.1-P.B)
　　　For the sake of your father, I....

Furthermore, as stated earlier, the distant haplology refers to the merging of the preposition zai in a preverbal locative with the imperfective marker zai of the main verb of the sentence in the absence of an aspectual suffix of the verb or any auxiliary element indicating futurity. In the presence of any of such forms, a zai in a preverbal locative is a pure preposition.

The recognition of the imperfective aspect marker zai and the terminal aspect marker Zero is crucial to the analysis of the two locatives. In the absence of an aspectual verb suffix, a preverbal locative marks the imperfective aspect as well as denotes the location of a durable or repetitive, active action or an habitual activity. A postverbal locative denotes the location of a static position or presence, including the static state of affairs at the termination of an abrupt action or transition.

The proposed explanation of the functional difference between the two locatives serves as a powerful rule which generates only grammatical sentences. It also constitutes a criterion for eliminating ungrammatical sentences such as (1a, 2a, 3b), etc., which none of the previous studies is able to do.

Tai defines the function of postverbal locatives as locating the participant affected. He regards the difference between the place adverbials in (46a) and (46b), a minimal pair in English, as that, while the place adverbial in (46b) modifies the action, the place adverbial in (46a) modifies the recipient, i.e. a noun (Tai 1975:175-6, and fn. 17).

(46a)　John keeps his car in the garage.
(46b)　John washes his car in the garage.[4]

I would define keep as [-active], and wash as [+active]. To be precise, verbs such as keep, leave, put, etc, designate actions consisting of an active inception followed by a durable inactive continuum. In other words, these verbs denote a {+ →-active} process in reality. Verbs such as wash, polish, build, on the other hand, designate actions which are [+active] throughout the whole course of their occurrence. This difference in the nature of the verbs, in my opinion, is the essential distinction between (46a) and (46b). And, in both sentences, the place adverbial modifies the verb.

4.　See Tai (1975:175-176 and footnote 17), Fillmore (1968:26 and footnote 34).

*　An earlier version of this paper was published in 1977 under the title of 'the Two Aspect Markers Hidden in Certain Locatives' (Chen 1977).

REFERENCES

CHAFE, Wallace L. 1970. *Meaning and the Structure of Language*. The University of Chicago Press.

CHAO, Yuan-ren. 1968. *A Grammar of Spoken Chinese*. University of California Press.

CHEN, Chung-yu. 1977. The two aspect markers hidden in certain locatives. *Proceedings of Symposium on Chinese Linguistics, 1977 Linguistic Institute of the Linguistic Society of America*. Student Book. Taipei.

CHOMSKY, Noam. 1965. *Aspects of the Theory of Syntax*. MIT Press.

FILLMORE, Charles. 1968. The case for case, *Universals in Linguistic Theory*, E. Bach and R. Harms, eds. New York: Holt, Rinehart and Winston. Pp. 1-88.

HUANG, Shuan-fan. 1974. Mandarin causatives. *Journal of Chinese Linguistics* 2.3: 354-369.

JACKENDDFF, Ray S. 1972. *Semantic Interpretation in Generative Grammar*. MIT Press.

LAKOFF, George. 1970. *Irregulariity in Syntax*. New York: Holt, Rinehart and Winston.

LI, Charles N. and Sandra A. THOMPSON. 1974. Co-verbs in Mandarin Chinese: verbs or prepositions? *Journal of Chinese Linguistics* 2.3: 257-78.

LI, Y.C. 1974. What does 'disposal' mean? Features of the verb and noun in Chinese. *Journal of Chinese Linguistics* 2.2: 200-18.

MCCAWLEY, James D. 1968. The role of semantics in grammar. *Universals in Linguistic Theory*, E. Bach and R. Harms, eds. New York: Holt, Rinehart and Winston. Pp. 125-70.

TAI, James. 1975. On two functions of place adverbials in Mandarin Chinese. *Journal of Chinese Linguistics* 3.2/3: 154-79.

TENG, Shou-hsin. 1975. Predicate movements in Chinese. *Journal of Chinese Linguistics* 3.1: 60-75.

WEINREICH, Uriel. 1966. Explorations in semantic theory. *Current Trends in Linguistics III*.

ON PREDICATIVE COMPLEMENTS

Abstract.

    Both characters 得 and 的 have been used to represent the particle in what Chao calls 'predicative complements' in sentences such as <u>Ta zou de kuai</u>. Inconsistencies have been found in the syntactic analyses (by Chao and Gao Ming-kai, for instance) of constructions containing predicative complements, which indeed have arisen from the non-uniformity of usage concerning the character for the particle and the subsequent confusion. This paper attempts to prove, through internal structural evidence as well as cross-dialect comparison, that the true identity of the particle involved is 得, which differs from the potential particle 得 in both its syntactic behavior in questions and its phonological representation with respect to stress. After a transitive verb, both the predicative particle 得 and the nominalizer 的 may occur. This is, perhaps, the source of the previous confusion. Chao's predicative complements, complements of extent, and resultative complements (in V-R compounds) are ultimately reduced to the same underlying structure, 'complements of result or extent'. When the complement is a sentence or a verb carrying a scalar notion (such as 'half-dead', 'slow'), particle 得 which signals the meaning 'to the effect/extent that' occurs between the main verb and the complement (e.g., <u>Ta qi de bansi</u>). When the complement is a verb carrying a categorical notion (such as 'dead', 'finished'), no particle occurs in between (e.g., <u>Ta qi si le</u>).

0. Introduction.

Chao (1968) makes a distinction between two major types of complements in verb-complement constructions. One is a predicative complement (as in (1)); which, according to Chao, is a free form.

(1)　他走的很慢。(Chao 1968:350)
　　　(The way, speed, etc.) he walks is very slow.

The other one is a bound verb-complement compound as in

(2)　我吃飽了。(Chao 1968:350)
　　　I have eaten full - I am full from eating.

This paper begins with a quest for the true identity, i.e., the graphic representation, as well as the syntactic function of the particle de in a predicative complement. This paper also questions the validity of the free vs. bound distinction between predicative complements and V-R (resultative) compounds as postulated by Chao, and ultimately proves that Chao's predicative complements, V-R compounds, and complements of extent can all be reduced to the same underlying structure.

1. Particle de in Predicative Complements vs. the Nominalizer 的.

As Chao points out, there is no uniformity concerning the character involved in a predicative complement being 的 or 得. For instance, Chao uses 的 for this particle and Gao Ming-kai (1971) uses 得. (It ought to be pointed out that in Chao's book, p. 357, lines 9 and 11, character 得 was used in a predicative complement, and 的 was used in a potential complement. That is apparently a mistake in writing.)

Concerning its syntactic function, Gao analyzes (3a) and (4a) as Subj + Pred constructions, with the particle de forming part of the subject. In line with such an analysis, he interprets (3a) and (4a) as abbreviated forms of (3b) and (4b) respectively, with the nominal expression deleted.

(3a) 他來得 快。 (Gao 1971:8)
      Subj.   Pred.

(3b) 他來的速度 快。 (Gao 1971:8)
      The speed he came was fast. (Gloss mine)

(4a) 他說得 真好。 (Gao 1971:8)

(4b) 他說的話 真好。 (Gao 1971:8)
      What he said was really good. (Gloss mine)

Gao maintains that the 得 in (3a, 4a) is indeed the same 的 as in (3b, 4b) (Gao 1971:8; "其實這種'得'就是規定詞的'的'.").

The inconsistency in his analysis is self-evident. For if this were the case, why did he not use 的 in sentences (3a) and (4a)? The fact that he adhered to character 得 in these sentences indicates that he did recognize a difference, although he was not able to grasp it in full.

Chao, who uses character 的 to represent this particle, is caught in a dilemma when analyzing such constructions.

(5a) 你唱的好聽。 (Chao 1968:357)

He states that in rendering (5a) as 'The way (manner, etc.) you sing is beautiful', the translation seems to commit the IC analysis to

(5b) 你唱的 好聽。 (Chao 1968:357)

and yet the feeling of the native seems to prefer the analysis

(5c)　　你 唱的好聽。　(Chao 1968:357)

He then adopts a solution suggested by Li Fang-kuei as given in (5d).

(5d)　　　　　　唱的　　好聽
　　　　　你　　Subj. 2　Pred. 2
　　　　　Subj. 1　　Pred. 1
As for you, the way of singing is beautiful.

A problem arising from such a Subj + Pred analysis of the V-predicative complement constructions, as pointed out by Chao himself, will be discussed later.

Both Gao and Chao analyze the particle <u>de</u> as forming part of the subject. It is, thus, a nominalizer in both treatments. Gao uses 得 to represent the particle in a predicative complement and Chao uses 的. Before coming to a conclusion, in the following discussion I shall simply use <u>de</u>.

I believe that the inconsistency or dilemma in each of the two analyses has arisen from the confusion of a true nominalizer 的 and the homophonous particle in a predicative complement whose identity is now being questioned. In Cantonese and the Shanghai dialect, for example, the particle in a predicative complement shares the same form with the potential particle 得 in its phonological as well as graphic representations. Corresponding to the nominalizer 的 in Mandarin, Cantonese has 嘅 [kɛ] and the Shanghai dialect has 格 [kɤʔ]. The following cross-dialect comparison aims at unveiling the distinction in Mandarin which has been obscured by homophony and the subsequent non-uniformity of usage with respect to the character chosen.

Type A: containing a nominalizer:

(6 'What you have done is correct; what he has done is not correct.'
 a) Cantonese : 你做嘅對，渠做嘅唔對。
 b) Shanghai : 儂做格對，伊做格弗對。
 c) Mandarin : 你做 de 對 他做 de 不對。

(7 Did he like what you wrote?'
 a) Cantonese : 你寫嘅渠中唔中意？
 b) Shanghai : 儂寫格伊阿歡喜？
 c) Mandarin : 你寫 de 他喜歡嗎？

Type B: containing a predicative complement:

(8 'You did it right, he did it wrong.'
 a) Cantonese : 你做得對，渠做得唔對。
 b) Shanghai : 儂做得對，伊做得弗對。
 c) Mandarin : 你做 de 對，他做 de 不對。

(9 'Did you write it fast?'
 a) Cantonese : 你寫得快唔快？
 b) Shanghai : 儂寫得快弗啊？ /儂寫得快弗快？
 c) Mandarin : 你寫 de 快嗎？ /你寫 de 快不快？

Type C: containing a potential particle:

(10 'If you can do it right, we'll go.'
 a) Cantonese : 你做得對，我哋就去。
 b) Shanghai : 儂做得對，阿拉就去。
 c) Mandarin : 你做 de 對，我們就去。

(11 'Can you write fast?'
 a) Cantonese : 你寫唔寫得快？

    b) Shanghai：儂阿寫得快？
    c) Mandarin：你寫 dé 快嗎？/ 你寫 dé 快，寫不快？

    The above cross-dialect comparison clearly indicates that the particle in a predicative complement ought to be 得. While the distinction between predicative complements and potential complements, both involving the particle 得, may be neutralized in statements (8a-c vs. 10a-c), it is clearly manifested in questions (9a-c vs. 11a-c). In Mandarin, the particle 得 of a predicative complement differs phonologically from the potential particle 得 in that while the latter may be stressed in careful speech, the former is never stressed. The contrast involved in the following pairs of sentences sufficiently supports the distinction made here.

    (12   做得好嗎？
        a) Zuo dé hao ma?
           Can you finish it (by tomorrow)?

        b) Zuo dě hao ma?
           Is it well done?

    (13   洗得干净嗎？
        a) Xi dé ganjing ma?
           Can it be washed clean? (Can the dirt be removed?)

        b) Xi dě ganjing ma?
           Is it clean? (Has it been washed clean?)

    There is an important difference between the predicative particle 得 and the nominalizer 的 with respect to distribution. The predicative particle 得 occurs after both transitive and intransitive verbs; the nominalizer 的 occurs after transitive verbs only. I shall substantiate this point first with evidence in Cantonese and Shanghai:

(14a)　　我走得快。
　　　　 Cantonese, Shanghai, Mandarin:
　　　　 I walk fast.

(14b)　　Cantonese: *我走嘅快。
　　　　 Shanghai: *我走格快。
　　　　*What I walk is fast.

Hence, Mandarin: *我走的快 (Cf. Gao's choice of the character in 3a).

Let us turn to the structural evidence within Mandarin. While sentence (4b), which contains a transitive verb, can be transformed into questions like (4c) and (4d), sentence (3b), which contains an intransitive verb, cannot be transformed in the same ways:

(4c)　　這(話)是他說的嗎?
　　　　 Was this said by him?

(4d)　　這是誰說的(話)?
　　　　 Who said this?

(3c)　　*這(速度)是他來的嗎?
　　　　*Was this the speed he came with?

(3d)　　*這是誰來的(速度)?
　　　　*Who came with this speed?

These examples clearly indicate that while ta shuo de hua, which contains a transitive verb, can be abbreviated to ta shuo de; and ta lai de sudu, which contains and intransitive verb, cannot be abbreviated to ta lai de. In other words, particle de in sentences which contain an intransitive verb (e.g. 14a) has only one possible identity or interpretation; that is, the predicative particle 得.

As a matter of fact, the inconsistency in each of the aforementioned analyses readily supports my claim. Gao's sentence (4a) is indeed a mixture of (4e), which contains an abbreviated noun phrase (as signaled by the nominalizer 的), and (4f), which contains a predicative complement.

 (4a) 他說得 真好。(Gao 1971:8)
 (4e) 他說的 真好。←(4b) 他說的話 真好。
    Subj. Pred.
    What he said was really good.
 (4f) 他 說得真好。
    Subj. Pred.
    He said it very well.

Chao was also dealing with two different types of constructions in his discussion of sentence (5a). The first one, (5b), contains a nominalizer; the second one, (5c), which ought to be re-written as (5c'), contains a predicative complement proper.

 (5c) 你 唱的好聽。 (Chao's analysis)

 (5c') 你 唱得好聽。 (Proposed analysis)

Thus the two types of constructions are distinguished in (15a) and (15b).

 (15a) Constructions containing an abbreviated NP (and the nominalizer 的).
   你唱的 (歌) 好聽。
   他說的 (話) 很對。
   他畫的 (畫) 還不錯。
   他抄的 (數字) 都錯了。
   他買的 (衣服) 最貴。

(15b) Constructions containing a predicative complement (and the predicative particle 得).

你　　　唱得好。
我　　　走得快。
還是　他　　寫得最好。
　　　他的字　寫得漂亮。

To sum up, two different types of constructions which have hitherto been obscured and confused because of homophony of the particles involved and the subsequent non-uniformity of usage with respect to the characters chosen are now differentiated.

In the following discussion, I will use character 得 for the particle in a predicative complement, even when quoting Chao's examples.

2. Predicative Complements, V-R Compounds and Complements of Extent.

Chao distinguishes two types of Verb-Complement constructions: Free predicative complements as in (1') and bound V-R compounds as in (2).

(1')　　他走得很慢。

(2)　　我吃飽了。

It is found that the distinction of free vs. bound is not valid because the V-R compounds are not always bound. In <u>chi bao</u>, for example, both constituents are free and versatile (16-19). Moreover, it can also be expanded to a V-predicative complement construction as in (20).

(16)　　我吃了。
　　　　I've eaten.

(17)   我吃够了。
       I've had enough.

(18)   我飽了。
       I'm full.

(19)   我看飽了。
       I've seen enough of it.

(20)   我吃得很飽了。
       I'm quite full.

Therefore, I suggest that the distinction be replaced by the presence vs. absence of the particle 得.

Chao raises a problem in his discussion of predicative complements (21a-d; Chao 1968:358, stress marks mine):

(21a) 你擺歪了。
       You have set it crooked.

(21b) 我擺不正嘞。
       But I can't set it straight.

(21c) 那麼他怎麼擺得正呢?   (得: can be stressed)
       Then, how come he can set it straight?

(21d) 那麼他怎麼擺得正呢?   (得: unstressed)
       Then how come he set it straight?

The structures of the underlined portions in these four sentences, as given by Chao, are:

(21a)   a V-R construction
(21b)   a potential construction
(21c)   a potential construction
(21d)   a Subj-Pred construction

Chao recognizes that such an analysis of sentences (21a-d) spoils the parallelism of constructions in the four sentences. But then he says there is nothing incredible about parallel ideas not being paralleled by their linguistic expressions.

In the previous section I already rejected the analysis of predicative complements into a Subj-Pred construction. I have also pointed out that the formal difference between a predicative complement and a V-R compound lies in the presence vs. absence of the particle de. In the following discussion, I shall prove that the presence or absence of the particle de is predictable, hence, predicative complements and V-R compounds are indeed the same structure.

Furthermore, I shall also prove that it is superfluous to distinguish between Chao's predicative complements and his complements of extent (as in 22).

(22)   冷得要命。
       It's terribly cold.

Chao was probably compelled to make such a distinction because he had mistakenly used the character 的 for the particle in predicative complements in the first place.

In the following discussion on structural relationships between the verb and the complement, I recognize only the formal distinction, i.e., the presence vs. absence of a 得 in between.

3. A Semantic Classification of the Complement and the Presence of Particle de.

It has been pointed out that the formal difference between a predicative complement and a V-R compound lies in the presence vs. absence of particle de. On this basis, I shall try to reduce the two constructions to the same underlying structure.

Three patterns are recognized in the structural relationships between a verb and a complement :

Pattern A: <u>V + Comp</u>: the complement follows the verb immediately; the (predicative) particle <u>de</u> cannot occur in between. E.g.,

  (23) He got it. (He hit the target.)
  a) 他丢中了。
  b) *他丢得中了。 (得: unstressed; predicative comp.)

 Cf: a potential complement,
  (23b') 他丢得中了。 (得: can be stressed)
   Now he can hit the target.

Pattern B: <u>V + Comp</u>
    <u>V de + Comp</u> / <u>V de + hen Comp</u>:
the complement follows the verb with or without the (predicative) particle <u>de</u> in between. When <u>de</u> is present, an adverb <u>hen</u> may be required. E.g.,

  (24a) 他氣瘋了。
    He was furious.

  (24b) 他氣得瘋了。
    He was so infuriated that he went mad.

  (25 He has made it clear.
  a) 他説清楚了。
  b) *他説得清楚了。 (得: unstressed; predicative comp.)

Cf: a potential complement,
- (25b') 他說得清楚了。 (得: can be stressed)
   Now he can make it clear.

- (25c) 他說得很清楚了。
   He has made it very clear.

- (25d) 他說得清楚。
   He made it clearer (then she did). (Predicative comp.)
   He can make it clear. (Potential comp.)

Pattern C: <u>V de + Comp</u>: The complement cannot occur immediately after the verb; particle <u>de</u> is an obligatory element.

(26 He was infuriated almost to death.
- a) *他氣半死。
- b) *他氣半死了。
- c) 他氣得半死。

When more examples are listed and compared, a correlation between a certain feature of the complement and the presence or absence of the particle <u>de</u> emerges.

Verb	Complement	Structural Patterns			Notion Carried by the Complements	
		V + Comp	V <u>de</u> + Comp	V <u>de</u> + <u>hen</u> Comp	Categorical	Scalar
餓 'be hungry'	死了 'dead'	+	−	−	+	−
打 'hit'	破了 'broken'	+	−	−	+	−
丢 'throw'	中了 'got it'	+	−	−	+	−

Verb	Complement	Structural Patterns			Notion Carried by the Complements	
		V + Comp	V de + Comp	V de + hen Comp	Categorical	Scalar
做 'do'	完了 'finished'	+	−	−	+	−
走 'walk'	錯了 'astray'	+	−	−	+	−
弄 'manipulate'	壞了 'out of order'	+	−	−	+	−
跌 'fall'	斷了 'broken'	+	−	−	+	−
說 'say'	清楚了 'clear'	+	−	−	+	−
掃 'sweep'	干淨了 'clean'	+	+ (no le)	+	+	+
來 'come'	晚了 'late'	+	+ (w or w/o le)	+ (no le)	+	+
吃 'eat'	飽了 'be full'	+	+	+	+	+
氣 'be angry'	瘋了 'mad'	+	+	−	+	+
等 'wait'	膩了 'tired'	+	+	+	+	+
擺 'put'	歪了 'crooked'	+	+	+	+	+
唱 'sing'	好聽 'beautiful'	−	+	+	−	+

Verb	Complement	Structural Patterns			Notion Carried by the Complements	
		V + Comp	V de + Comp	V de + hen Comp	Categorical	Scalar
走 'walk'	快/慢 'fast/slow'	−	+	+	−	+
餓 'be hungry'	半死 'half-dead'	−	+	−	−	+
畫 'paint'	像 'resemble'	−	+	+	−	+
冷 'cold'	要命 'terribly'	−	+	−	−	+
睡 'sleep'	舒服 'comfortable'	−	+	+	−	+
寫 'write'	潦草 'in a cursive way'	−	+	+	−	+

The above comparison reveals that if the complement carries a categorical notion (such as 'dead', 'finished', etc.), it occurs immediately after the verb; if the complement carries a scalar notion (one which is a matter of degree, such as 'half-dead', 'slow', etc.), particle de must appear in between. The validity of the distinction made between categorical and scalar notions can be proved by the fact that the change-of-state particle le appears only after a categorical notion (in fact, its appearance is obligatory) but not after a scalar notion. This is precisely because no categorical change of state is involved in a scalar notion. Since a scalar notion is a matter of degree, particle de is there to signal the relation 'to the effect that' or 'to the extent that'.

Complements which are marked [+categorical] and [+scalar] may occur in all the patterns because they are susceptible to two interpretations. For instance, qingchu 'clear' could mean either 'to have included all the necessary information' (hence, a categorical notion) or 'to be very explicit and meticulous about all the details' (hence, a scalar notion). Ganjing 'clean' could either mean 'all the unwanted items have been removed' (hence, categorical) or 'clean' (hence, scalar). Wan 'late' taken deictically is a categorical notion; taken relatively it is a scalar notion. As a scalar notion, wan 'late' does not occur with the change-of-state particle le, for, unlike the cases with other members in this group, there could not have been stages in which the person first came not so late, then later, until it was very late. With all the other complements of this group, le is optional when adverb hen is present. Obviously finer distinctions are needed to account for the different behaviors of these complements in the pattern V de + Comp. I shall, however, leave this question open.

Now it has been shown that the formal distinction between Chao's predicative complements, V-R compounds, and complements of extent lies in the presence vs. absence of the particle de, which in turn correlates with the scalar vs. categorical notions conveyed by the complements. Therefore, formally the three types of constructions can be reduced to the same underlying structure (27a), and I propose the term 'complement of result or extent' to embrace the three constructions.

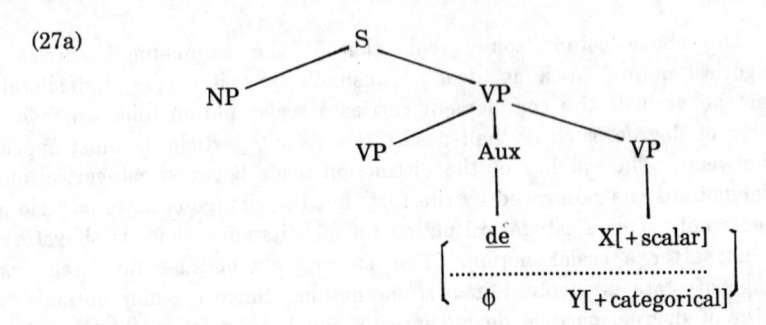

(27a)
```
              S
           /     \
         NP       VP
               /  |  \
             VP  Aux  VP
                  |    |
                  de   X[+scalar]
                  φ    Y[+categorical]
```

Lacking formal distinction, it is superfluous and insignificant to distinguish between complements of extent and complements of result, especially as the two sometimes may not be differentiated even semantically. For instance, the complements in (28) and (29) below can be said to be expressing either result or extent.

In his discussion of the nominalizer 的, Chao analyzes the nominalizer in (28) as expressing 'result or extent'.

(28) 收音機吵的我聽不見你說話了。 (Chao:1968:296)
The radio is so loud that I can't hear you talk.

Furthermore, in his treatment of complements of extent, Chao gives the following example:

(29) 你老叫，叫得我心慌。 (Chao 1968:355)
You keep calling, it makes me nervous.

I see no justification for his choice of two different particles (hence, the two different structural interpretations) for apparently the same meaning or function. It is my opinion that the particle de in (28) is not a nominalizer, but the particle expressing, as Chao says, 'result or extent'. That is, the same 得 as in (29). The 'complements or result or extent' may also appear in the following form, structure (27b).

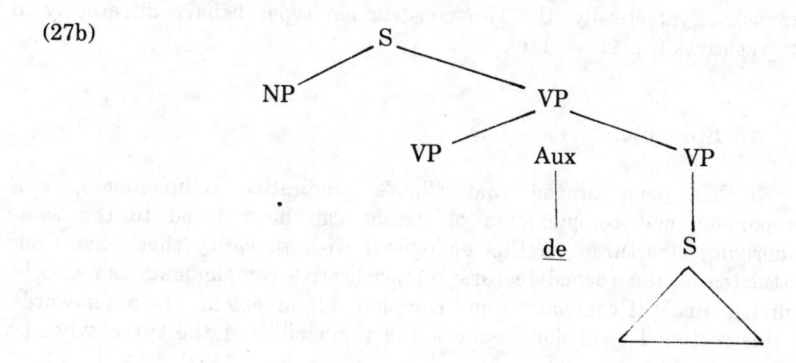

(27b)

```
            S
           / \
         NP   VP
             /|\
           VP Aux VP
              |   |
              de  S
                 /_\
```

－51－

Now it has been proved that Chao's predicative complement is not a Subj-Pred construction, but a V-R∼E (result or extent) construction. The parallelism of constructions in the four sentences, (21a-d), is restored.

4. Conclusions.

It has been substantiated through internal evidence as well as cross-dialect comparison that the particle in Chao's predicative complements ought to be 得, instead of 的.

The free vs. bound distinction between predicative complements and V-R compounds cannot be maintained, because there is no justification for the term 'compound'. Chao's predicative complements, resultative complements (in V-R compounds) and complements of extent are reduced to the same underlying structure, 'complements of result or extent'. When the complement is a clause or a verb carrying a scalar notion, particle 得 which signals the meaning 'to the extent that', 'to the effect that', occurs between the verb and the complement. When the complement is a verb carrying a categorical notion, no particle occurs in between. Phonologically, this particle of result or extent differs from the potential particle in that while the latter may be stressed in careful speech, the former is never stressed. Syntactically, the two construction types behave differently in interrogatives (Cf. 9c vs. 11c).

5. An Epilogue.

It has been proved that Chao's predicative complements, V-R compounds, and complements of extent can be reduced to the same underlying structure. In this epilogue I wish to verify that what Chao postulates as the formal features of predicative complements can also be found in his V-R compounds and complements of extent. In other words, in this section I shall double-check the reducibility of the three syntactic types.

The first formal feature of predicative complements as postulated by Chao is that there can be a pause or pause particle after <u>de</u> as is the case after other kinds of subjects (30a).

(30a) 你唱的嘿，— 太響， (Chao 1968:356)
As for (the way) you sing, (it is) too loud.

In my earlier discussion it has been shown that when talking about predicative complements, Chao was in fact dealing with both predicative complements and constructions involving the nominalizer 的. In saying "...as is the case after other kinds of subjects", he was obviously dealing with the nominalizer 的. It is, therefore, necessary to find out whether or not this pause may occur after the 得 particle of a predicative complement proper. To avoid confusion with the nominalizer, I shall again resort to comparison with other dialects where the two particles are phonetically different.

(30b) Cantonese: 你唱得咧，— 太大聲。
(30c) Shanghai: 儂唱得嘿，— 忒響。

As verified by sentences in Cantonese and the Shanghai dialect, pause is also possible after the predicative complement particle 得. Sentences (31) and (32) indicate that this formal feature can also be found in Chao's V-R compounds (31) and complements of extent (32).

(31) 我吃得啊，— 半飽。
As for me, I'm only half full.

(32) 他高興得啊，— 哭起來了。
He was so very happy that he cried.

Incidentally, Chao (1968:356) maintains that there are two cases in which pause is not permitted after <u>de</u>: the cases with <u>duo</u> (as in <u>hao de duo</u> 'much better') and <u>hen</u> (as in <u>hao de hen</u> 'very good'). Chao's explanation of this is that duo and hen do not often occur as single morpheme predicates. However, I wish to present a different view: duo and hen here are not predicative complements; they are adverbs intensifying the predicate complement hao. This point can easily be substantiated by the following examples:

(33a) 你唱得好。
        V. Comp.

(33b) 你唱得好很。
        V. Comp.
        You sang it (very) well.

(34a) 你比他唱得好。
        V. Comp.

(34b) 你比他唱得好得多。
        V. Comp.
        You sang it (much) better than be did.

The whole phrases hao de hen (= hen hao) and hao de duo function as predicative complements in (33b) and (34b). The first de in these two sentences is what Chao calls a particle of predicative complement, and pause after it is possible as shown in (33c) and (34c).

(33c) 你唱得啊，— 好得很。
        You sang it — ah — quite well.

(34c) 你比他唱得啊，— 好得多。
        Compared with his singing, you sang it — ah — much better.

The second formal feature of predicative complements is that adverbs may be added before the complement, as in

(35) 我唱得不太好聽。 (Chao; 1968:356)
I don't sing very well. (Gloss mine)

(36) 他寫得又快又清楚。 (Chao 1968:356)
He writes rapidly and clearly. (Gloss mine)

Sentences (37) and (38) illustrate that this feature can also be found in Chao's V-R compounds and complements of extent.

(37) 我吃得不太飽。
I'm not very full (from eating).

(38) 他高興得又哭又笑。
He was so happy that he cried and laughed (at the same time).

The third formal feature of Chao's predicative complements is that in interrogative constructions it is the complement that appears in the V-bu-V form, that is, the interrogative begins after de (39) (whereas with the potential constructions, the interrogative appears in the action verb, that is, before de, as in 9c vs. 11c).

(39) 你走得快不快？
Do you walk fast?

Again, this feature can also be found in his V-R compounds

(40) 看，我擺得正不正？
Look, did I set it straight?

(41) 他傷得厲不厲害？ /他傷得厲害不厲害？
Was he badly hurt?

It has now been illustrated that all the three formal features of Chao's predicative complements are also found in his V-R compounds and complements of extent. This in turn justifies the reduction of the three construction types into one, complements of result or extent. Nevertheless, this does not amount to claiming that these formal features can be found in all the V-R compounds or complements of extent. Rather, it merely shows that these formal features do not constitute a barrier to the reduction of the three construction types, as they were postulated, presumably, to distinguish between predicative complements and potential constructions. Moreover, these 'formal features' are not always free of interference from non-formal features. For example, both <u>lihai</u> and <u>yaoming</u> in (42a) and (43a) are complements of extent, yet they behave differently with regard to the third formal feature mentioned above (42b vs. 43b):

(42a) 加拿大冷得厉害。
(43a) 加拿大冷得要命。
It is extremely cold in Canada.

(42b) 加拿大冷得厉不厉害？ /加拿大冷得厉害不厉害？
(43b) *加拿大冷得要不要命？ /*加拿大冷得要命不要命？
Is it extremely cold in Canada?

REFERENCES

CHAO, Yuen Ren. 1968. *A Grammar of Spoken Chinese*. University of California Press.

CHEUNG, Samuel Hung-nin. 1972. *Cantonese as Spoken in Hong Kong*. The Chinese University of Hong Kong Press.

GAO, Ming-kai. 1971. 漢語語法論集. Hong Kong: Chungwen Shuju (崇文書局).

LU, John H-T. 1977. Resultative verb compounds vs. directional verb compounds in Mandarin. *Journal of Chinese Liguistics* 5.2.276-313.

PEKING UNIVERSITY. 1964. *Hanyu Fangyan Cihui* (漢語方言詞匯). Peking.

CONSTRAINTS ON THE 'V1-ZHE···V2' STRUCTURE

ABSTRACT.

The structure 'V1-zhe··· V2' is a grammatical frame which is subject to specific semantic constraints. When the subject is the agent for two [+ active] actions occurring at the same time, this structure presupposes the following: (1) The two actions denoted are interrelated in certain ways; (2) One of the actions is the predominant and the other is the subordinate; this relative weighting is reflected in the fixed order of the two verbs.

Contrary to the common assumption or description that this structure marks "two actions that occur simultaneously", the great majority of the sentences of this type involve only one active action at one time on the part of the subject. The structure, 'yibian V1··· yibian V2', on the other hand, is compatible only with separable events. The differences between the two structures neutralize when the two events denoted are interrelated yet separable.

0. Introduction.

In some previous discussions of the 'V1-zhe··· V2' structure, examples such as (1a) and (2a) below (and others) have been found. However, such sentences are not well-formed because they violate a subtle syntactic-semantic constraint.

(1a)　他吃着飯說話。　(J. C. Thompson 1968:75)
　　　He talks while eating.

(2a)　我吃着飯唸書。　(Ross 1984:16)
　　　I am eating as I study.

And because of the same constraint, sentence (3a) admits only one reading rather than being theoretically ambiguous, as has thus been claimed (J. C. Thompson 1970:63).

(3a)　關着門喝酒。

This paper sets out to explore that constraint and in the meantime identify certain finer distinctions which may not have revealed themselves very clearly under the common assumption or description of "two actions that occur simultaneously" (J. C. Thompson 1968; and others given in different words).

1. Two [+active] Actions on the Part of the Subject.

1.1. Constraint 1-A: Interrelationship.

(4a)　他拍着桌子罵人。
　　　He was striking the table while berating the man.

(5a)　*他擦着桌子罵人。
　　　He was cleaning the table while berating the man.

(6a)　他拍着手唱歌。
　　　He clapped his hands (in rhythm) while singing.

(7a)　*他打着字唱歌。
　　　He typed while singing.

(8a)   他扶着欄杆下樓梯。
       He walked down the stairs with his hand on the banisters (for support).

(9a)   *他看着書下樓梯。
       He was reading as he walked down the stairs.

(10a) 他吹着口哨下樓梯。
       He whistled while walking down the stairs.

(11a) 我們看着指揮唱。
       We watched the chorus master as we sang.

(12a) 他揮着手説再見。
       He waved his hand as he bade us good-bye.

(13a) 他甩着手走過去。
       He was swinging his hands as he walked over (to the other side).

(14a) 我看着電視上的示范做體操。
       While watching the demonstration (of aerobics) over television, I imitated accordingly.

(1a)   *他吃着飯説話。

(2a)   *我吃着飯唸書。

(15a) *她做着功課看孩子。[1]
       She was doing her homework as she looked after the kid.

---

1. Cf. a sentence of similar surface structure:

The sentences above are derived from the same structure and each involve two [+active] verbs to which the subject is the agent. Yet, some of them are well-formed and acceptable while others are not. What are the reasons for that?

On a closer look, however, we are able to see a difference between the two groups of sentences: While a certain interrelation can be established between the two actions in the well-formed sentences, no such interrelation is conceivable between those in the ill-formed ones. These interrelations can be classified into three categories: (1) Conventional: Actions interrelated through frequent co-occurrences, they have a complementing relationship (e.g. 4a, 6a, 12a); (2) Logical: Actions interrelated through necessity, they have an interdependent relationship (e.g. 8a, 11a, 14a); (3) Physical: Actions involving different body parts and occurring at the same time, they are either in coordination or non-interfering (e.g. 10a, 13a), although it is sometimes not easy to draw a line between the two. (See Section 4 for closeness of relationship by category as reflected in syntactic behavior.)

Actions which are not apparently interrelated can only appear in the 'yibian V1 ⋯ yibian V2' (or, 'yimian V1 ⋯ yimian V2') structure, which presumes no particular relationship between the two actions. Hence, the following well-formed sentences:

  (5b) 他一邊擦桌子，一邊罵人。
  (7b) 他一邊打字，一邊唱歌。
  (9b) 他一邊看書，一邊下樓梯。
  (1b) 他一邊吃飯，一邊說話。

←   她看着孩子做功課。
  (i) * She was looking after the kid as she did her home work. (看: kān)
  (ii) She watched the kid doing his homework. (看: kàn)

This sentence is well formed in reading (ii). But it is then a pivotal construction in which N2 is both the object of V1 and subject of V2.

(2b)　　我一邊吃飯，一邊唸書。

(15b)　　她一邊做功課，一邊看孩子。

Having discriminated between the presence of a semantic presupposition of an interrelation between the two verbs in the structure 'V1-zhe...V2' and the lack of it in 'yibian V1 ⋯ yibian V2', we are able to appreciate the difference between sentences (14b) and (14c) below: The person was watching an exercise program in (14b) but not in (14c).

(14b)　　我看着電視做體操。
　　　　　I watched television and did the exercise (as demonstrated).

(14c)　　我一邊看電視，一邊做體操。
　　　　　I did my exercise while watching television (--a way for better utilization of my precious time).

Li and Thompson (1981:223-5) maintain that in the 'V1-zhe ⋯ V2' construction, the event of V1 provides a durative or on-going background for the event of V2. This claim is not always valid when both of the verbs denote [+active] actions. In most of the well-formed sentences discussed above (e.g. 4a, 6a, 8a, 10a, 13a), the events of the V2's seem to be providing a durative background for the events of the V1's instead of the other way round. For instance, when we say a person was striking the table while berating someone, it is more likely that the berating (i.e. the event of V2) occurred incessantly and the striking of the table occurred intermittently rather than the other way round (Cf. Section 2.2.1.).

1.2.　Constraint 1-B: Predominant vs subordinate in weighting.

(16a)　　*他唱着歌跳舞。

(16b)　　*他跳着舞唱歌。
　　　　　He was singing and dancing (at the same time).

(1a)   *他吃着飯說話。(Cf. 53a)

(17a)   他嚼着口香糖說話。
He was chewing gum as he talked.

The previous section concludes that the structure 'V1-zhe ⋯ V2' presupposes a certain interrelation between the two verbs. Now *singing* and *dancing* (16a & b) are actions which often co-occur as well as complement each other. Yet, put in either order, the two sentences are equally unacceptable. On the other hand, both (1a) and (17a) contain two verbs denoting movements which take place in the oral cavity, but one is acceptable while the other is not. How can these discrepancies be accounted for?

It seems that the two actions even though interrelated, have to be of unequal weighting in terms of their occupation of the agent's physical and/or mental involvements. In other words, it has to be one principal action accompanied by another action which is less demanding on the agent's physical energy and/or mental concentration.

Both *singing* and *dancing*, or *eating* and *talking*, require considerable amount of energy and concentration from the agent; therefore, these pairs of actions cannot enter into this structure. On the other hand, *chewing gum* requires far less concentration compared to *talking*, hence, (17a) is acceptable. And obviously V2 signals the principal action. This relative weighting is further confirmed by the fact that the order of the two verbs is unalterable, as shown in the examples below:

(4b)   *他罵着人拍桌子。
(6b)   *他唱着歌拍手。
(8b)   *我下着樓梯扶欄杆。
(11b) *我們唱着看指揮。
(13b) *他走着過去甩手。

(17b)　　*他說着話嚼口香糖。

　　Summing up this section, when the subject is the agent for two active actions occurring at the same time, this structure presupposes the following: (1) The two actions are interrelated in a certain way; (2) The two actions are of unequal weighting in terms of their occupation of the agent's physical and mental involvements.

2. One [+active] Action on the Part of the Subject.

　　The sentences in the ensuing discussion are not subject to the interrelation constraint because the subjects are engaged in one active action only.

2.1. V1 denoting states.

2.1.1. V1 denoting state of affairs of the external world.

　　(3a)　　開着門喝酒。
　　　　　　To drink behind closed doors.

　　(18)　　他開着燈（～窗戶～收音機～冷氣）睡覺。
　　　　　　He slept with the light (～window～radio～air-conditioner) on (/open).

　　In the above sentences, the V1's denote the state of affairs of the external world, and the agents are engaged in one dynamic situation only.

　　Verbs such as <u>kai</u> 'open; switch on' and <u>guan</u> 'close; switch off', etc., contain in themselves both the active inceptive motion and the inactive resultant state of affairs (Chen 1978).

　　J.C. Thompson (1970:63) claims that sentence (3a) is theoretically ambiguous because it can also be read as 'to drink while closing the door'.

Actually, no such ambiguity would arise from it. When these verbs are taken as active motions, i.e. in their first phase, sentences (3a) and (18) would not meet with the 'interrelation' constraint, because the occurrence of one of the actions (*drinking, sleeping*) provides no ready or logical anticipation of the other (*closing the door, switching on the light*). If one does not want to be seen drinking, he drinks after the door is closed rather than 'while closing the door'. If sentence (3a) could be interpreted as 'while closing the door', sentence (18) would also mean 'He slept while switching on the light'. Similarly, we would have to accept sentence (19b) as well:

(19) 他開着門睡覺。
    a) He slept behind closed doors.
    b) *He slept while closing the door.

To say that a person was drinking while closing the door, one would probably express it by (3b) or (3c), if there were a number of doors to close.

(3b) 他一邊關門，一邊還喝了一(～幾)口酒。
He managed to take a (few) sip(s) while closing the door.

(3c) 他一邊關門，一邊喝酒。
He was drinking while closing the doors.

2.1.2. V1 denoting state of the subject in relation to an external dynamic situation.

(20a) 他吹着電扇睡覺。
He slept with the fan on.

(21a) 我淋着雨一路跑來。
I ran all the way here in the rain.

(22) 我曬着太陽等了老半天。
I have been waiting for a long time in the sun.

The V1's in these sentences are [+active], yet they denote the state of the subject, which is consequential upon an external dynamic situation. The subject is only being exposed to the effect of V1 and is not playing any active role in respect to it. It is, therefore, a patient rather than an agent to V1.

2.1.3. V1 denoting state of body parts.

    (23)   别光着脚跑来跑去。
               Don't run around barefooted.

    (24a)   你空着手去吃饭?
               Are you going to the dinner party empty-handed?

    (25)   她穿着大衣跳舞。
               She danced in her overcoat.

    (26)   他蒙着眼睛弹钢琴。
               He played the piano blindfolded.

In sentences (23, 24a) the V1's involve no apparent actions on the part of the subject. In sentences (25, 26), chuanzhe and mengzhe each denote the resultant state of an action which has already been completed (and the subject may or may not have been the agent for that action). The subjects are engaged in one action only, which is denoted by V2.

2.2. Only one physical action is being realized between V1 and V2.

2.2.1. One manifestation for two verbs: indivisibility.

    (27a)   他竖着耳朵听。
               He pricked up his ears (and listened).

(28) 他睜大着眼睛看。
He watched with wide eyes.

(29) 她尖着嗓子叫。
She screeched, thus stretching her vocal cords (to their utmost limit).

(30) 他搶着回答。
He beat the others in his offer of the answer.

(31) 他忙着倒茶。
He was busy serving teas.

(32) 別只顧着說話 (忘了看路)。
Don't be so engrossed in talking (and forget to watch your step).

(33) 我幫着她追那個人。
I helped her chase after that man.

Sentences (27a-33) each contain two verbs, yet there is but one physical manifestation; the two situations denoted by the verbs are virtually indivisible. In sentences (27a-29), V1 cannot occur without the unavoidable effect or result of V2. In sentences (30-33), V1 depends on V2 for its actual realization. In other words, V2 embodies the action/situation of V1, and V1 could not have independent existence from that of V2.

In situations like these, neither of the verbs can be said as providing a durative background for the event of the other verb (Cf. Section 1.1).

Ross (1984:16) claims that the insertion of -zhe is only possible if the first verb of a two-verb sequence is an action or event that can occur independently of the other verb. The examples here point quite to the contrary.

2.2.2. V2 referring to situation to be realized at a later time.

(34)　你等着瞧！
　　　"You just wait and see!"

(35a)　她鬧着要買大衣。(Li and Thompson: 223)
　　　 She made a fuss about wanting to buy a coat.

(36)　留着喂狗。(Zhu: 164)
　　　Save it for the dog.

The V2's in these sentences indicate the goal or purpose of V1, which is to be realized at a later time. Moreover, the action of V1 will conclude as soon as V2 takes effect.

Zhu has pointed out that the V2 in (36) indicates purpose.

2.2.3. V2 indicating spontaneous effect of V1.

(37a)　我騎着脚踏車追他。
　　　 I chased after him on my bike.

(38)　我騎着脚踏車兜風。
　　　I went for a spin on my bike.

(39)　說着玩兒的。
　　　(I) only said it for fun.

(40)　他擋着路不讓人過。
　　　He blocked the way and wouldn't let any one pass.

The sentences here are similar to those of Section 2.2.2 in that the V2's also indicate the purpose of V1. However, while the V2's there are expected to be realized at a later time, the V2's here indicate a spontaneous effect of V1. The sentences here also resemble those in Section 2.2.1 in that the realization of one verb is embodied in that of the other. However, the pairs of verbs here lack the interdependency exhibited in the pairs of verbs there. In the sentences here, the V1's may exist without the purpose and, subsequently, the effect of V2; the V2's may also materialize in actions other than that of V1 (See Chen 1986, for actions that have non-specific and multi-formed realizations). For instance, other than cycling, one can chase after someone, zhui, by running or driving a car; one can also go for a spin, doufeng, in a car or on a boat.

Zhu has pointed out that the V2 in (39) indicates purpose.

2.2.4. V1 indicating orientation or affiliation of the action of V2.

(41) 別當着孩子的面吵架。
Don't quarrel in front of the children.

(42) 他對着鏡子做鬼臉。
He made faces before the mirror.

(43) 順着這條路走。
Follow this road.

(44a) 他們繞着公園跑。
They jogged round the park.

(45) 照着我的話做！
Do as I tell you!

(46) 她跟着他去了。
She went along with him.

(47) 爺爺領着孫子上動物園。 (Zhu:63)
Grandpa took his grandson to the zoo.

(48)　　他帶着一幫人到處跑。(zhu: 63)
　　　　He's been to everywhere, leading a group of his men.

In sentences (41-46), V1 describes or prescribes the orientation, i.e. position or direction, of the action of V2. In sentences (47,48), V1 denotes a situation which accompanies the action of V2. Moreover, the realization of that situation is manifested in no specific actions other than that of V2. Hence, in all the sentences above, the agents are involved in only one physical action.

Unlike the cases in 2.2.1, where the realizations of V1 and V2 are virtually indivisible, the V2's here are able to deviate from the prescription imposed by the V1's, should the agents choose to do so.

Zhu has pointed out that the V1's in (47, 48) convey the meaning of 'accompanying action'.

3. V1 Is a [-active] or [(+→)-active] Verb Denoting Body Postures.

(49)　　她低着頭笑。
　　　　She smiled looking down.

(50a)　 他站着吃飯。
　　　　He was eating standing.

(51a)　 他躺着看書。
　　　　He was reading a book lying down.

(52)　　他們提着燈籠散步。
　　　　They took a walk carrying a lantern.

(53a)　 別含着一口飯説話 (Cf. (la))。
　　　　Don't talk with a mouthful.

(54a) 他叼着根烟走進來。
He walked in with a cigarette dangling from his lips.

(55a) 捧着金碗討飯。
"Holding a gold bowl to beg for food."

The term 'body posture' here refers to both the less complicated postures such as *standing, lying, (sitting)* etc. and the more complicated ones in which a part of the body is sustaining an object in an inactive manner, as in (52-55a).

The present inactive posture may have resulted from an earlier active inceptive motion such as zhan qi lai 'stand up', tang xia (qu) 'lie down', ti qi (lai) 'lift up', etc. At the moment of speaking, the action has already completed the active inception and entered into a static phase, which will remain until another active action occurs to change it. The inactive posture may also be a section of a durative inactive action, of which the inception has to be activated by another action which is active. For instance, in order to hold something in the mouth in the manner of han or diao (as in 53a, 54a), one has to put it in first.

Unlike verbs such as cazhe (zhuozi) 'cleaning (the table)', dazhe (zi) 'typing', which necessarily involve active movements, the transitive verbs discussed here, such as tizhe 'carrying', hanzhe 'keeping in the mouth', pengzhe 'holding', etc, are inactive in their physical modality (Cf. Section 4.3). These verbs per se do not connote active movements; if any movements occur in the course of *holding, carrying*, etc., these movements are accidental rather than inherent.

Here, a minor point concerning the aspect marker -zhe is to be injected. Chen (1978:84) proposes that zai is an imperfective marker and can indicate both actions in actual progress and habitual activities, whereas -zhe, a progressive marker, can only indicate actions in progress. Using examples (50b, 51b), Tsai (1981:88) claims that -zhe can also indicate habitual activities.

(50b)　他喜歡站着吃飯。
　　　　He likes to eat standing.

(51b)　他總是躺着看書。
　　　　He is always reading books lying down.

Actually, the meaning of habitual activity in these examples is expressed lexically rather than syntactically. Stripped of xihuan 'like to' and zongshi 'is always', respectively, the two remaining sentences (50a, 51a) are devoid of the meaning of an habitual activity.

4.　'V1-zhe…V2' and 'yibian V1…yibian V2'-- a Comparison.

The discussion in Section 1 has shown that the structure 'yibian V1…yibian V2' (hereafter, structure Yi-) is the frame for two unrelated actions that occur simultaneously. Let us see whether sentences which involve only one active action on the part of the subject (i.e. those in Sections 2 and 3) and sentences which involve two interrelated actions (i.e. the well-formed sentences in Section 1) can also be converted into structure Yi-. For this purpose, one or two sentences from each subsection will be chosen for comparison.

4.1.　V1 denoting states.

(2.1.1)　(3d)　　*他一邊開着門，一邊喝酒。
(2.1.2)　(21b)　*我一邊淋雨，一邊（一路）跑來。
　　　　(20b)　　他一邊吹電扇，一邊睡覺。
(2.1.3)　(24b)　*我一邊空着手，一邊去吃飯。

The examples above reveal that structure Yi- is not applicable to sentences involving one (or two) static state of affairs (e.g. 3d, 24b) (Cf. Section 2.1.1, 3b and 3c).

Both (21b) and (20b) involve a dynamic situation in respect to V1, however, (21b) is ill-formed because the subject was an involuntary recipient of the effect of V1, and in engaging in V2, there was no escape from the effect of V1. In other words, the subject has chosen to engage in one action only, but was involuntarily and inevitably affected by the external dynamic situation. In that sense, the V1 and the V2 are inseparable situations. Sentence (20b) is well-formed because V1 and V2 are separable; the subject has chosen to have both occur at the same time. This point can be exemplified by the contrast between (21b) and (56), where V1 and V2 may each exist without the other but were chosen to be realized at the same time. Moreover, when V1 denotes a state that has no bearing on a dynamic situation (e.g. 3d, 24b, as contrasted with 21b, 20b), the presence of -zhe is obligatory.

(56)　　我一邊淋雨，一邊吃冰淇淋。
　　　　I ate ice-cream in the rain.

In sum, when V1 denotes the state of the subject, which is consequential upon an external dynamic situation, structure Yi- is compatible so long as that state and the subject's action in respect to V2 are separable events. This structure cannot apply when V1 denotes a static state of affairs that has no bearing on a dynamic situation.

4.2. Only one action being realized at one time.

(2.2.1.)　(27b)　*他一邊豎(着)耳朵，一邊聽。
(2.2.2.)　(35b)　*她一邊閙，一邊要買大衣。
(2.2.3.)　(37b)　*我一邊騎脚踏車，一邊追他。
(2.2.4.)　(44b)　*他們一邊繞公園，一邊跑。

The examples here again show that structure Yi- is not compatible with situations involving only one action at one time.

4.3. V1 denoting body postures.

(53b)　＊別一邊含着一口飯，一邊説話。

(54b)　＊他一邊叼着根烟，一邊走進來。

(55b)　＊他一邊捧着金碗，一邊討飯。

(51 　他一邊躺着，一邊看書。
c)　＊He was reading a book lying down.
d)　He was reading a book while lying on bed. (The doctor advises him to lie on his back for at least two hours during the day.)

In sentences (51C, 53b-55b), the V1's denote an inactive body posture along which V2 takes place. The sentences involve only one action and hence cannot occur in structure Yi-. However, structure Yi- is applicable if the body posture denoted by V1 has a purposeful existence apart from being one of the possible manners in which V2 is realized. That is, the two events are separable, as in the case of (51d).

4.4. Two interrelated actions.

Conventional --complementing:

(4c)　他一邊拍桌子，一邊罵人。
(6c)　他一邊拍手，一邊唱歌。
(12b)　他一邊揮手，一邊説再見。

Physical--coordinating or non-interfering:

(10b)　他一邊吹口哨，一邊下樓。

(13c) 他一邊甩手，一邊走過去。

Logical--interdependent:

(8c) *我一邊扶欄杆，一邊下樓梯。

(11c) *我們一邊看指揮，一邊唱。

(14   我一邊看電視上的示范，一邊做體操。
- d) *I was watching a demonstration (on exercise) over television as I did my exercise.
- e) I was watching a demonstration (on cooking) over television as I did my exercise.

    The comparison here reveals that structure Yi- is applicable when the interrelation between the two actions is loose, i.e. the two are still separable, as in the cases of the conventional and the physical categories. This is where the compatibilities of the two structures overlap. Structure Yi- is not applicable when the interrelation is a close one, i.e. the two are interdependent and hence inseparable, as in the cases of the logical category. This point can be verified by sentences (14e) and (57) below, both involving unrelated actions. Nevertheless, two interdependent actions which are to materialize alternately become separable actions, and hence compatible with structure Yi- (58, as opposed to 11b).

(57) 我們一邊看那些漂亮女孩，一邊唱。
We were looking at those pretty girls as we sang.

(58) 我們一邊看食譜，一邊做。
We kept referring to the cookbook as we prepared the dish.

5. Conclusion.

    The discussions above reveal that contrary to the common assumption or description that the 'V1-zhe ⋯ V2' structure marks "two actions that occur simultaneously", the vast majority of the sentences involve only one active action on the part of the subject at one time. When it does involve two active actions on the part of the subject, there are certain constraints. The structure 'yibian V1 ⋯ yibian V2', on the other hand, is compatible only with separable events. The differences between the two structures neutralize when the two events denoted are interrelated yet separable.

The categorization of situations involving one or two active actions for the two opposing structures in this discussion is by no means thorough. However, the proposed constraints should hold for new submissions as well.

Many of the contrasting examples in Section 4 are illustrations of the same verbs in the same structural frame differing in their intended realizations and emerging different as to category and hence grammaticality.

Chu (1984) maintains that there is a middle ground in grammatical categorization as well as between the notions of grammaticality and ungrammaticality, and linguistic indeterminacy arises due to different organization of concepts by individual speakers. This is indeed very true. But I should think that once a common conceptualization of a given situation or event is reached, there should be no middle ground left in the dichotomy of grammatical vs ungrammatical; any indeterminacy would mean that certain aspectual or semantic distinctions are still to be discovered and captured. This should at least be a necessary working assumption. A provision in terms of 'context' should be recognized as a theoretical working parameter to account for the deviant materializations of a verb under deviant situations (Cf. Chen 1986, 'context' and 'mutation in aspectual character'). It is possible that our differences here are more apparent than real; I may be saying the same thing to a different degree.

REFERENCES

CHEN, Chung-yu. 1978. Aspectual Features of the Verb and the Relative Positions of the Locative. *Journal of Chinese Lingusitics* 6.1: 76-103.

CHEN, Chung-yu. 1982. On the Time Structure of English Verbs. *Pappers in Linguistics* (Canada) 15.3: 181-90.

CHEN, Chung-yu. 1986. On the Physical Modality of English Verbs. *Pappers in Linguistics* (Canada) 19.2: 131-53.

CHU, Chauncey Cheng-hsi. 1983. *A Reference Grammar of Mandarin Chinese for English Speakers*. New York and Bern: Peter Lang Publishing, Inc.

CHU, Chauncey Cheng-hsi. 1985. Lu's Syntactic Word and Conceptual dynamism. *Journal of the Chinese Language Teachers Association* 20.1: 9-38.

COMRIE, Bernard. 1976. *Aspect*. Cambridge University Press.

LI, Charles N. and Sandra A. Thompson. 1981. *Mandarin Chinese: A Functional Reference Grammar*. University of California Press.

ROSS, Claudia. 1984. Grammatical Categories in Chinese. *Journal of Chinese Language Teachers Association* 19.2: 1-22.

THOMPSON, J. Charles. 1968. Aspect of the Chinese Verb. *Linguistics* 38: 70-76.

THOMPSON, J. Charles. 1970. Aspect of the Chinese Verb: A Supplemental Note. *Linguistics* 60: 63-68.

TSAI, Shu-shu. 1981. Verbal Aspect: A Contrastive Analysis of Mandarin and English with Pedagogical Implications. Unpublished Ph.D. dissertation. The University of Texas at Austin.

ZHU, Dexi (朱德熙). 1982. 語法講義。商務印書館。北京。

STEMMING FROM THE VERBAL SUFFIX -ZHE

0. Foreword.

Chauncey C. Chu (1987) sees a philosophical or methodological dissimilarity between him and me in terms of approach. However, there is another fundamental dissimilarity between us, which lies in our intuitions of the Chinese language. Differences in language intuition are not easily reconcilable. Fortunately, both his paper and mine focus on approaches and technicalities rather than acceptabilities of certain sentences. This paper begins as a reply to Chu, but subsequently questions for him also arise.

1. Semantic Constraints or Pragmatic Constraints.

I have proposed (Chen 1986) a twofold semantic constraint on the grammatical frame 'V1-zhe...V2'. That is, when the subject is the agent for two [+active] actions occurring at the same time, this structure presupposes the following: (1) The two actions denoted are interrelated in certain ways (the interrelationship can be categorized as conventional, logical and physical)[1]; (2) One of the actions is the predominant and the

---

1. (1) Conventional: Actions interrelated through frequent cooccurrences; they have a complementing relation. (2) Logical: Actions interrelated through necessity; they have

other is the subordinate; this relative weighting is reflected in the fixed order of the two verbs. At the same time, I have also pointed out that the majority of the sentences of this structural frame involve only one active action at one time on the part of the subject.

Chu contends that the constraints I have proposed are "largely pragmatic rather than semantic". His first reason is that conventional, logical and physical relationships are subject to modification or change if the pragmatic situation alters. (His second reason pertains to the notion 'weighting', which will be dealt with in the next section.)

Chu uses the following sentences to illustrate his point (the first five sentences mine; " √ " to mean 'acceptable', and "*", 'unacceptable'):

(1a)　他拍着桌子罵人。(Chen & Chu: √)
　　　He was pounding on the desk while berating the man.

(1b)　他擦着桌子罵人。(Chen: *; Chu: √)
　　　He was cleaning the table while berating the man/others.

(2a)　他吹着口哨下樓梯。(Chen & Chu: √)
　　　He walked down the stairs whistling.

(2b)　他看着書下樓梯。(Chen: *; Chu: √)
　　　He was reading as he walked down the stairs.

(3a)　我們看着指揮唱。(Chen & Chu: √)
　　　We watched the chorus master as we sang.

← an interdependent relationship. (3) Physical: Actions involving different body parts and occurring at the same time; they are either in coordination or non-interfering, although it is not always easy to draw a line between the two.

(3b)　我們摸着機器唱。
　　　　We felt the machine as we sang.

　　Sentence (3b) was proposed by Chu as a counter-example for my constraint. It was to depict a situation in which a group of blind men felt (the vibration of) a machine to sense the rhythm beat of the music when they sang. This sentence turns out to be a good supporting example for my constraint, because it expounds very clearly what I meant by a logical interrelation, which is an interdependent relationship: The act of singing has to rely on the feeling of the beat of the music, hence the interrelation requirement is met.

　　In my earlier paper, sentences (1a, 2a, 3a) served to illustrate conventional, physical and logical interrelations, respectively; (1b, 2b) were examples of semantically ill-formed sentences, as no such interrelations were apparently conceivable between the two actions denoted. Chu argues that "with a slight stretch of situation, a practical, if not as natural, interpretation can be easily obtained." He maintains that (1b) would sound very well-formed describing what a child would do when he is made to clean the table while the other family members are enjoying themselves.

　　I would say that Chu's interpretation is quite a natural one. Moreover, there is no need to "stretch" the situation at all. In fact, the situations for (1b) and (2b), as well as all the sentences marked as unacceptable in my earlier paper, are entirely possible and probable; yet the utterances are still unacceptable. That is what grammatical errors mean. To enter into this particular frame, the two actions must be interrelated, not in some or any way, but in a certain way. The pounding of the desk and the berating in (1a) are interrelated through frequent cooccurrences in many cultures. It is thus an "established" relationship, hence characterized as "conventional". The seeming cause-and-effect relation between the cleaning of the table and the berating in (1b), on the other hand, is purely and merely fortuitous.

　　My constraint of interrelation is not to be interpreted in terms of coherence in human behavior, which, I think, is Chu's understanding (or misunderstanding) of my constraint. Rather, it refers to certain relationships which this grammatical structure presupposes. Sentences (1b) and (2b), therefore, should have been expressed in a different structural frame. Hence, what the boy in Chu's description was doing is

(1c) 他一邊擦桌子，一邊罵人。

And an answer to Chu's question "How did he fall?" could be

(2c) 他一邊看書，一邊下樓梯，

which may very well incur the comment "It served him right,"

(2d) 活該，誰叫他一邊看書，一邊下樓梯！

(2d') 活該，誰叫他邊走邊看！

In my earlier paper I have provided several contrasting examples to illustrate how the same pair of verbs differing in their intended realizations may emerge different as to interrelationship and hence grammaticality in the same structural frame (Chen 1986:18). I shall recall just one pair of examples here:

(4 我看着電視上的示范做體操。
    a) While watching the demonstration (on exercise) over television, I imitated accordingly.
    b) *While watching the demonstration (on exercise) over television, I did my exercise accordingly.

(5 我一邊看電視上的示范，一邊做體操。
    a) I was watching a demonstration (on cooking) over television as I did my exercise.
    b) *I was watching a demonstration (on exercise) over television as I did my exercise.

Chu maintains that if a slight alteration of the non-linguistic environments makes the otherwise unacceptable sentences acceptable, then the problem involved can hardly be regarded as semantic. Here, let me make use of an analogy to elucidate the situation:

On the subject of the determination of the sex of a fetus, it has been claimed that the food which the prospective mother has taken may affect the selection and hence combination of the chromosomes from the XX and XY pairs. Even if this is possible, we cannot say that the sex of the fetus is determined by the food the mother takes, it is still the combination of the chromosomes that determines the sex. Similarly, alterations in the pragmatic situation may change the interrelationship between the two actions denoted by the verbs and make them eligible or ineligible for entering into a particular structural frame; but eligibility itself still hinges on the interrelationship, which is semantic in nature.

Pragmatic situations are ever-changing. To speak of a "pragmatic constraint" is to speak of a formulation of behavioral variables, which amounts to speaking of an open-ended and free-for-all constraint. In other words, a "constraint" that has no binding force at all. I, therefore, contend that only semantic constraints are valid constraints. As has been stated in my earlier paper (Chen 1986:18), a provision in terms of 'context' should be recognized as a theoretical working parameter to account for the deviant materializations of a verb under deviant situations. Contexts or pragmatic situations are variables that may change the aspectual character of a verb or the interrelationship between the actions denoted and hence change the eligibility; but they are not the constraint itself.

2. 'Weighting' versus 'Saliency'.

2.1. The parameter 'weighting' in my framework.

The second part of my twofold constraint is that the two actions even though interrelated, have to be of unequal weighting in terms of their occupation of the agent's physical and/or mental involvement. In other words, it has to be one principal action accompanied by another action which is less demanding on the agent's physical energy and/or mental concentration. This constraint explains the unacceptability of sentences (6a, b), (7a, b) below, in which the two actions denoted require relatively the same amount of energy and/or concentration. Moreover, this relative weighting is reflected in the fixed order of the two verbs, as can be exemplified by (8a) as opposed to (8b).

(6a) *他唱着歌跳舞。
(6b) *他跳着舞唱歌。
He sang and danced (at the same time).

(7a) *他吃着飯說話。
(7b) *他說着話吃飯。
He ate/talked while talking/eating.

(8a) 他嚼着口香糖說話。
He was chewing gum as he talked.

(8b) *他說着話嚼口香糖。
He was talking as he chewed gum.

Chu's first point of disagreement is that sentences (6a, b) and (7a) (and presumably (7b), (8b) too) don't have to be unacceptable.[2] He maintains (in his Note 14) that sentence (7a) is appropriate for depicting a person who does not usually talk except when eating, (6a) is appropriate for describing a dancer, and (6b), a singer. Since it is clear that acceptability would not be a profitable line of argument between us, I shall not dwell on this point any longer except for calling his attention to an old and familiar expression in our language, "載歌載舞", which when rendered

---

2. In his Note 14, Chu states that Ma (1985: 42) gives (6a) as an acceptable form. To this, I can also point out that at the CLTA Annual Meeting, 1985, wherein my earlier paper was presented, no one raised any doubt regarding the ill-formedness of (6a) as well as all the other sentences marked with "*". In fact, the session chairman even told me that all my examples were very convincing.

colloquially is "邊唱邊跳"; both forms happen to exhibit a coordinate, rather than subordinate, relationship.

Chu's second contention is "her claim about weighting doesn't hold for her own examples", meaning examples (9a, b):

(9a) *她看 (ㄱ) 着孩子做功課。³
(9b) *她做着功課看 (ㄱ) 孩子。
She does her homework while baby-sitting.

Chu maintains that sentence (9a) should by my principle of weighting be easily acceptable because baby-sitting is much less strenuous, at least mentally, than doing homework. (Well, try to baby-sit a two-year old toddler!) Sentence (9b), according to Chu, is a perfectly well-formed answer to "Why do you not like her to baby-sit for you?"

Here let's examine the technicality of my constraint. As has been stated in my earlier paper, my constraint is twofold; the actions denoted have first to be interrelated in certain ways before they can be compared on weighting. "Doing homework" and "baby-sitting" cannot pass the first screening, therefore, are not even eligible for comparison. Hence, my claim holds very well. Thus, a well-formed answer to the question mentioned above should be (9c) or (9c'):

(9c) 她一邊做功課，一邊看孩子。
(9c') 她一邊看孩子，一邊做功課。

2.2. The parameter 'saliency' in Chu's framework.

In connection with 'weighting', Chu has made the following claims:

---

3. Read as "她看(√) 着孩子做功課," this sentence becomes an acceptable pivotal construction, meaning 'She watches the child doing his homework.'

(1) "Perhaps, weighting is best regarded as a process of conceptual organization where more salient happenings or situations are coded in the principal structures and lesser ones, in subordinate structures. Narrowed down to narrative discourse, they correspond to foregrounding and backgrounding, respectively. "(Chu: Section 3.1.B) (2) "Cognitively, an action is inherently more salient than a process (including durative), which is in turn inherently more salient than a state." (Chu: Section 2) (3) "We feel quite comfortable to conclude that the discourse/pragmatic function of -zhe is to serve as a backgrounding device." (Chu: Section 3.1.B) There remain, it seems to me, a few doubtful points.

2.2.1. With verbs of the same order.

In Chu's cognition, there is an inherent order of saliency in verbs: action > process > state. How are we to decide which verb is more salient (whatever the definition of this term), then when both verbs denote actions, or for that matter, states? Take the first and the last verbs on Chu's (Section 1.6) 'active--stative' scale, 繞 and 對, as examples:

(10a) 他繞着公園跑。
(10b) ?他跑着繞公園。
He ran around the park.

(11a) 他對着鏡子發呆。
(11b) ?他發着呆對鏡子。
He was in a daze, staring blankly into the mirror.

Now, in (10a, b), both V1 and V2 denote actions, and in (11a, b), states. Can we say that both orders, (10a) and (10b); (11a) and (11b), are acceptable, since the two verbs are equal in terms of saliency? Certainly not! Hence, a mere order of priority in terms of verbal categories for the determination of saliency is inadequate.

2.2.2. Validity of the order.

My second submission here concerns the validity of Chu's order of saliency, i.e. action > process > state, in relation to backgrounding and foregrounding. Take a sentence from Li and Thompson (1981: 223) as an example,

(12) 她鬧着要買大衣。
　　　She made (/is making) a fuss about wanting to buy a coat.

V1 here, 'to make a fuss about; to make a noise; to make a scene', denotes an action; V2, 'wanting to buy a coat', denotes a psychological state. Here, there is an action, supposedly more salient, appearing as the background and a state, less salient, as the foreground.

To furnish another example, the verbs 哭 'cry' and 逃 'escape' are classified as denoting action and process, respectively, in Teng's (1975: 163, 165) analysis. In sentence (13) below, however, the action, which is supposedly more salient than the process, turns out to serve as the background.

(13) 她哭着逃出去。
　　　(Escaping from the room,) she ran out crying.

Thus, Chu's order of saliency by verbal category once more reveals its inadequacy.

2.2.3. Backgrounding vs foregrounding.

On the claim that the discourse/pragmatic function of -zhe is to serve as a backgrounding device, there are two doubtful points: (1) Does the verb affixed with -zhe necessarily denote an action/event that is less salient and hence provide the backgrounding information? In sentence (12), "making a fuss" is what is physically going on; "wanting to buy a coat" is an invisible psychological state and is the cause or motive for the physical happening. It runs contrary to our intuition to say that the motive, i.e. the invisible psychological state, is more 'salient' and is the foreground, and the physical noise and, possibly, actions are less salient and constitute the background. In other words, the claim that suffix -zhe is necessarily, or always, a backgrounding device is questionable.

(2) Does every sentence necessarily contain backgrounding and foregrounding information, granted that there are two verbs? Let us examine sentences (14a), (15) and (10a) (Chen 1986):

(14a)　他搶著回答。
He beat the others in his offer of the answer.

(15)　我騎著腳踏車兜風。
I went for a spin on my bike.

(10a)　他繞著公園跑。
He ran around the park.

The two verbs in (14a) share one physical manifestation; V2 embodies the action/situation of V1, and V1 could not have independent existence from that of V2. In (15), V2 denotes a spontaneous effect of the action of V1. If we take away the 'foreground', V2, from sentence (14a), there simply can be no background, V1, left. And for sentence (15), take away the background, V1, there can be no realization of the foreground, V2. As for sentence (10a), would it be possible to circle the park without the action of running, or for that matter, cycling, walking? I, therefore, contend that when the denotations of the two verbs are virtually inseparable, there is no justification for differentiating between backgrounding and foregrounding. Hence, Chu's claim that suffix -zhe functions as a backgrounding device needs modification.

3. Over-simplification: Chu's Durative-Marking Function of -zhe and Its Subsequent "Neutralization".

3.1. Over-simplification: a "typical durative interpretation"?

After stating that the verbal suffix -zhe can be basically treated as a durative aspect marker, Chu proceeds to claim that whether in a simple or complex sentence, suffix -zhe occurring with an action verb renders itself a typical durative interpretation. This assertion seems to be unduly emphatic. Let's recall sentence (10a) again, wherein the verb 繞 is reckoned as an action verb by Chu (Section 1.6):

    (10a)   他繞着公園跑。
              He ran around the park.

Doesn't suffix -zhe, after the action verb "繞 — (公園)", call for a spatial or orientative, rather than durative, i.e. temporal, interpretation? Is there not a possibility of over-simplification in saying that -zhe signals a "typical durative interpretation"?

3.2. Neutralization: superimposition followed by subtraction?

Chu (Section 2.1) maintains that states are by nature durative, hence, the semantic durative-marking function of -zhe is in a way "neutralized" by the stativeness of the verb. The -zhe therefore only serves the syntactic function of subordinating the V-zhe structure to the main predicate. It seems that the function of -zhe has been unnecessarily narrowed down to that of a "durative marker" in the first place. And then, as required by circumstances, this function is said to be "neutralized". Is this not a case of adding on a superimposition and then subtracting it? Wouldn't it be more straightforward to say that suffix -zhe affords a range of meanings or relationships, which can be categorized into durative, spatial, orientative/directional (as in (16a, 17a) below), logical ((17a) again), etc.? Certainly this should be simpler than having to talk about cancellation, neutralization, enhancement and augmentation of semantic features later on (Chu: Section 4).

    (16a)   她跟着他走了。
              She went (along) with him.

(17a)　照着他的話做。
　　　　Do as he tells you.

Furthermore, Chu (Section 1.7) has asserted that with the action verb, -zhe serves to mark its durative aspect as salient (underscore original). With the posture and the placement verbs, the function of -zhe is to positively (underscore original) mark their durative aspect.

Posture verbs and placement verbs have a physical modality that can be characterized as [+ → -active] because they contain an active inceptive motion followed by a static state of affairs (Chen 1978). The second phase of such verbs is intrinsically durative. If the function of -zhe is to "positively mark" the durative aspect of the posture and the placement verbs, which are states in their second phase, then, why can't -zhe "positively mark" the durative aspect of state verbs too? Put another way, what has made this durative-marking function of -zhe survive the stativeness of the posture and the placement verbs, so that it has not been "neutralized"?

4. Over-differentiation.

4.1. Stative vs active for 照 and 跟.

Chu (Section 1.5) maintains that 照, as a verb is stative, 跟 as a verb is active: therefore, semantically -zhe is not so necessary for 照 as it is for 跟. I should think they belong to the same category (whatever category), and, semantically or syntactically, -zhe is not that necessary for 跟 either, as can be shown in the examples below. Hence, Chu's claim appears to be a case of over-differentiation.[4]

----
4. Likewise, contrary to Chu's (Section 2.1) claim, -zhe can also be deleted after 忙 (as in 忙倒茶). E.g.,

(16b)　她跟他走了。

(18b)　我跟他去 (買東西)。
　　　I went/am going with him (to do some shopping).

(19)　你跟我走。
　　　You come along with me./You follow me.

4.2. Subordinate reading and coordinate reading.

Chu also maintains that sentences (20a) and (21) are similar in that they can have either a subordinate reading or a coordinate reading, whereas sentence (22a) is straightforward and has only one reading.

(20a)　照他的話做。
　　　Do as he tells you. (Subordinate reading)
　　　Follow his words and do it. (Coordinate reading)

← 　(i)　領班：你還忙啊？你忙什麼噢？
　　　　跑堂：我忙倒茶，我忙端菜，我忙收錢，還不夠我忙的嗎？
　　(ii)　夫：你整天坐在家里，忙什麼忙？
　　　　妻：我忙燒飯啊，我忙洗衣啊，你那幫朋友來時我還忙倒茶，忙敬烟呢！
　　(iii)　兒歌：小蜜蜂，嗡嗡嗡，一天到晚忙做工....

(21) 照做。
Do according to (X). (Subordinate reading)
Follow (X) and do it .* (Coordinate reading)

(22a) 照着做。
Do it according to (X)./Do it accordingly.

The claim of "two readings", subordinate and coordinate, may very well be another instance of over-differentiation. For a coordinate reading to be established here, these utterances must allow alternatives with respect to V2 in terms of negation.[5]

(20b) *照他的話不做。
*Follow his words, but not do it.

(20c) 別照他的話做。
Don't do as he says.

---

5. A coordinate construction (without the presupposition of 'occurring at the same time', as in the structure '<u>yibian</u> V1...<u>yibian</u> V2') can be negated in respect to either V1 or V2. E.g.,

   (ia) 我不唱歌，只跳舞。
   (ib) 我(只)唱歌，不跳舞。

   A comparison of the positions of '做' will bring out the difference between the two sets of sentences below:

   (iia) 聽他的話，(別)做。
   (iib) 別聽他的話，快做。
   (iic) *聽他的話做。

   (iiia) 照他的話做，快回信。
   (iiib) 照他的話做，別回信。

   Hence, the stretch "照他的話做" does not afford a coordinate reading.

(20d)　　如果你不照他的話做,....
　　　　　If you do not follow what he says,....

The fact that sentence (20b) is not acceptable and that negation can only apply to V1 is a positive indication that sentence (20a) does not afford a coordinate reading. The underlying reason is that there involves only one action/event, rather than two separate actions/events. Likewise, sentences such as (10a) and (14a), which involve, not two, but one action/event cannot be negated with respect to V2. Hence, a coordinate reading would also be quite implausible for these sentences.

(10c)　　*他繞着公園不跑。
(10d)　　別繞着公園跑。
　　　　　He didn't/Don't run around the park.

(14b)　　*他搶着不回答。
(14c)　　別搶着回答。
　　　　　He didn't/Don't try to beat the others in offering an answer.

In this connection, sentence (22a), which Chu reckons as having only a subordinate reading, and sentence (16a), which should be a similar structure, cannot be negated in respect to V2 (e.g. 22b and 16c) either. This suffices a verification of the validity of the V2-Negation test for a coordinate reading.

(22b)　　*照着不做。

(16c)　　*跟他別走。
(16d)　　別跟他走。
　　　　　Don't go with him.

Hence, I contend that both sentences (20a) and (21) afford only a subordinate reading, just as (22a) does.

Finally, a few remarks on sentence (21) seem to be in order. Sentence (21) does accommodate two readings: The first one is what Chu calls the subordinate reading, "Do according to (X)". The second one, however, is not the coordinate reading which Chu sees in it. Rather, it is an idiomatic usage meaning "No matter what, I will do (X) all the same," which is an instance of the pattern "照 (樣) V".[6] This latter reading can be negated in respect to V2, as shown in (23) below, as idiomatic usages often rise above the constraint for the ordinary usages.

(23)   我要做的事，你不讓我做，我也照做(不誤)；我不要做的事，你要我做，我也照不做。
I'll do whatever I like, regardless of your opinion. But, what I don't feel like doing, even if you force me, I just won't do it.

5. Chu's Syntactically Defined Subordinate Verb in a Simple Sentence.

Chu (Section 2) objects to Ma's (1985) use of the term "semantic function" for the indication of subordination by -zhe. He maintains that it is a "syntactic function" because subordination is a structural notion rather than a semantic concept. A verb affixed with -zhe is thus said to be a subordinate verb. According to Chu, a subordinate verb in a simple sentence unambiguously indicates an unfinished utterance, and this is the reason for its necessary cooccurrence with particle ne, which, as described by Chu, serves an inter-sentential, rather than intra-sentential, function and is therefore a discoursal particle instead of a grammatical one. There remain a few perplexing points:

---

6.   Two more examples of the pattern '照 (樣) V':

    (i)   醫生不許他吃糖，可是他照(樣)吃 (or: 照吃不誤)。
    (ii)   "馬照跑，舞照跳。"

5.1. "Syntactic subordination".

Both particle ne and suffix -zhe (in simple sentences) are said to be indicating incompleteness of the sentence. If particle ne is reckoned as discoursal rather than grammatical in nature, why is the subordination signaled by -zhe necessarily a syntactic one? Can it not be semantic, or even discoursal, in nature? The only reason that Chu has given for this subordination to be syntactic is that "subordination is a structural notion." Is there not a chance that "subordination" is not the right choice of word in the first place? (Cf. Section 5.2 below) How syntactic subordination can be carried across the sentence boundary, whatever "complex operation" (Chu: Section 3.3) it might have gone through, still puzzles me.

5.2. "Unfinished sentences".

Chu's claim that simple sentences containing -zhe are unfinished is worth a closer look. Chu maintains that sentences such as (24, 25) below are not finished in the sense that they require something more to follow.

(24) 拿着！
Hold on to it!

(25) 湯熱着呢。
a) The soup is awfully hot.
b) The soup is being heated.[7]

---

7. Chu follows Chao's (1968: 249) interpretation and assigns two readings to this sentence. However, the (b) reading has apparently been left out in his later discussion. Reading (b), in fact, can do without ne. E.g.,

(i) 湯(在爐子上)熱着。

Incidentally, sentence (i), in which [durative] is expressed by the suffix rather than a preverbal marker, has a structural counterpart in Cantonese:

(ii) 湯熱緊。

Sentence (24), according to Chu, could imply or mean "it may be that you will find some use for it", or "you might drop it", etc. And sentence (25) could mean "I am positively/seriously asserting that the soup is hot, and for this reason you should do X". The fact that these sentences may have some implication or give rise to a certain anticipation does not necessarily make them unfinished statements as such. For instance,

(26) 快走！
Go quickly!/Hurry up!

(27) 我真的愛你。
I do love you.

(28) 明天一定會下雨。
It certainly is going to rain tomorrow.

The three simple sentences (26, 27, 28) here do not contain the suffix -zhe, nor the particle ne, and hence should be recognized as complete sentences/statements. Yet they may very well contain a deeper meaning or imply that "For this reason, you should do X." Sentence (26), for instance, could mean "Hurry, or we'll be caught," or "Move it, or else I'll heat you up!" Sentence (27) could imply "For this reason, you shouldn't forbid me to kiss you," or "I swear I do, although I can't marry you." For (28), "So, you might as well forget about your picnic," or "For this reason, give me back my umbrella!"

Chu's examples may be more implicit than mine. Yet, the difference is not significant enough to warrant a demarcation or categorization in terms of degree of implicitness or completeness. I therefore object to the use of the term "syntatic subordination" (or even "semantic subordination"), which is to mean that the sentence is syntactically (or semantically) incomplete, in reference to simple sentences containing -zhe. Sentences such as (24, 25) are syntactically complete because they contain all the necessary parts of speech as entailed by the verb. (Here I subscribe to Chafe's (1970) view of verb centrality.) They are also semantically complete because the message, at its face value, has been clearly delivered.

As to possible implicit messages such as "For this reason, you should do X", that is an area which is totally out of reach not only for the linguists, but, sometimes, for the hearer or even the speaker as well. A person with a one-track mind would probably take an utterance at its face value, even when hints have been provided, whereas an over-sensitive person may read more meanings than the speaker has intended for or would ever dream of. On the other hand, even if the hearer knows the speaker well, he may still be quite unsure of the speaker's intention or implication. Hence, "pragmatic interpretations" like these are too illusive for the linguists to hold on to as a basis for any formulation in general discussions.

Summing up this section, simple sentences that contain the verbal suffix -zhe are complete sentences, syntactically and semantically. The twang of incompleteness which Chu associates with such sentences can only be attributed to a discoursal nature, which could, perhaps, be better described as a "discoursal dependency", rather than a "syntactic subordination" as used by Chu.

6. Conclusion.

At the end of his paper, Chu says, "Another important point that I have been trying to make is that the interpretation of language structures, especially ones like aspect marker, is often incomplete if it is limited to the domain of one component of the language." Hence, as Chu says, his paper is intended to be a demonstration that, at least, for the durative aspect marker, syntax, semantics and pragmatics must be taken together to achieve a realistic description.

Chu's demonstration of integration of pragmatics into linguistic analysis is seen chiefly in two instances: (1) the pragmatic interpretations of "unfinished" utterances, i.e. simple sentences that contain the suffix -zhe, (2) the pragmatic constraint on the cooccurrence of the two verbs in the 'V1 -zhe...V2' structure. The pragmatic interpretation of an utterance may, in Chu's own words, vary widely. In fact, it is an open list, which is out of anybody's control, be it the linguist, the hearer or even the speaker (Cf. Section 5.2). It would, therefore, be dangerous to base a syntactic or semantic formulation/generalization on a few hypothetical "pragmatic interpretation". As for the "pragmatic constraint" for cooccurrence of verbs, it has been illustrated (Cf. Section 1) that alterations in the pragmatic situation may change the interrelationship between the two actions/events denoted by the verbs and hence the grammaticality of the sentence; they are, nevertheless, not the constraint itself.

Integration of pragmatics into linguistic analysis, in my view, can only be carried out on a sentence-specific basis, because pragmatic situations are ever-changing and formulation of behavioral variables is practically an impossibility. As has been pointed out in Section 1, a provision in terms of 'context' (i.e. pragmatic situations) ought to be recognized as a theoretical working parameter in semantic a well as syntactic formulations of any kind to account for the deviant materializations. In short, as far as the formulation of rules or constraints is concerned, integration of pragmatics into syntactic-semantic analysis cannot go far beyond the capacity of a stand-by provision.

On the other hand, the verbs of any utterance can only be correctly understood through a scrutiny of the physical realization of the actions denoted.[8] That is a pragmatic approach. The structural frame

---

8. The diagrams below delineate our conceptualization of the relationship between semantics and pragmatics:

Chu (p.c.) :   Chen:

'V1 -zhe...V2', for instance, had often, if not generally, been described as marking "two actions that occur simultaneously".[9] In my earlier paper, I pointed out with illustrations that the great majority of the sentences of this type involved only one active action at one time on the part of the subject. That was a distinct exemplification of integration of pragmatics into our understanding of the mode of materialization of specific utterances, which in turn leads to a better understanding of the grammatical structure concerned.

---
9. Thompson (1968); and others given in different wording.

REFERENCES

CHAFE, Wallace L. 1970. *Meaning and the Structure of Language*. University of Chicago Press.

CHAO, Y. R. 1968. *A Grammar of Spoken Chinese*. University of California press.

CHEN, Chung-yu. 1978. 'Aspectual Features of the Verb and the Relative Positions of the Locative.' *Journal of Chinese Linguistics* 6.1:76-103.

CHEN, Chung-yu. 1986. 'Constraints on the "V1-zhe...V2" Structure.' *Journal of Chinese Language Teachers Association* 21.1:1-20.

CHU, Chauncey C. 1987. 'The Semantics, Syntax and Pragmatics of the Verbal Suffix -zhe'. *Journal of Chinese language Teachers Association* 22.1.

LI, Charles N. and Sandra A. Thompson. 1981. *Mandarin Chinese: A Functional Reference Grammar*. University of California Press.

MA, Jing-heng. 1985. 'A Study of the Mandarin Suffix Zhe'. *Journal of Chinese language Teachers Association* 20.3:23-50.

TENG, Shou-hsin. 1975. *A Semantic Study of Transitivity Relations in Chinese*. Student Book Co. Ltd. Taipei.

THOMPSON, J. Charles. 1968. 'Aspect of the Chinese Verb.' *Linguistics* 38: 70-76.

REPLY TO A NOTE ON -ZHE

1. L. Mangione (1987) has tested 5 native speakers on the constraints I (Chen 1986a) have postulated on the 'V1-zhe...V2' structure. He obtained the following results:

Acceptance of sentences not conforming
to Chen's constraints

Sentence Subject	1	2	3	4
1	−	+	+	−
2	+	+	+	−
3	+	+	+	+
4	−	+	+	+
5	−	−	−	−

As the chart indicates, one informant (i.e. 20%) agreed to my constraints completely, three (60%) agreed partially, and one (20%) totally disagreed.

Mangione argues that my constraints are inadequate to account for some published materials and the subjective acceptability judgments of four native speakers. (He apparently has overlooked the fact that three of the remaining four native speakers still agreed to my constraints partially.)

Since no constraint can be adequate to account for both the '+' and the '−', it was illogical for Mangione to say that my constraints were inadequate. An accurate interpretation of the results should be: The inconsistencies yield a positive indication that certain subtle distinctions do exist in the language; such distinctions have apparently escaped some of the native speakers in varying degrees, but are certainly clear to others. My constraints have thus captured the intuition of the more restrictive speakers.

Moreover, in any acceptability test, the negatives have more significance than the positives, because people tend to indicate acceptance when they are unable to explain what seems to be wrong with the sentence. In studying the physical modality of English verbs, I have asked several native speakers about their intuition regarding the sentence "John has been keeping his car in the garage for the last ten minutes." (Chen 1986b) The informants were very uncomfortable about this sentence, yet finally they all chose to say that it was an acceptable sentence. Actually, this sentence does contain a violation to a subtle syntactic-semantic constraint;[1] the perfect continuous aspect when paired with a short time span anticipates that something active or physical has been going on, yet the verb *keep* is [-active] in physical modality. Hence, when an informant indicates acceptance, there is still a possibility that he is not really comfortable with the sentence, but he simply cannot explain what is wrong.

2. Mangione has cited as counterexamples certain sentences from some published materials.

(i) He states that a number of texts with a foreign learner orientation

---

1. This sentence may become acceptable when the verb keep changes it denotation from an inactive and unattended situation to a constructive, intense and, in that sense, dynamic continuum of a situation. It also becomes acceptable if the time span becomes long enough, because then the interpretation of an active commitment will automatically be filtered out and the interpretation of a habitual activity or a constant or perpetual state will come in (Chen 1986b).

contain sentences such as "他吃着飯看報", which would be viewed as counterexamples to my constraints. He has quoted from two such sources.

This is not surprising to me. It would be naive, on my part, to assume that all teaching materials are flawless. In the textbooks meant for the foreign learners, there are dialectal forms such as '棒子麵' ('corn flour'), peculiar expressions such as '美國飯' ('American food'), as well as ungrammatical sentences such as "他遇見一個老朋友的時候，他的老朋友就請他吃飯." ('When he met an old friend, his old friend invited him to eat.' Vol. 1, P. 171 of a certain textbook which was published in Taiwan, but the author was apparently residing in the U.S.) One or two blemishes, of course, would not reduce the usefulness of a book, especially when, most of the time, the teachers are able to point them out to the students.

However, peculiarities and ungrammaticalness do wear out. A teacher who has raised his eyebrow when he first encountered the expression '美國飯' may, after repeating it several times, come up quite naturally with '日本飯', '法國飯', '墨西哥飯', etc., as well. In substitution drills of syntactic patterns, it is particularly probable that certain finer semantic distinctions may slip through the fingers. The restriction imposed by the very limited employable vocabulary items may also foster the occurrence of sentences such as "吃着飯看報", "吃着飯說話".

Mangione has also cited an example, "……我們喝着談吧," [2] from an adapted text (Chen Q. 1972). I have asked several native speakers about their feelings towards this sentence. They all rejected it and said, "I would say '邊喝邊談' or '一邊喝一邊談'." One informant who holds a Ph.D. in Chinese literature commented that such a sentence appeared to be a reminiscence of the so-called translation style (翻譯體), which is deemed a non-Chinese style.

---

2. A seemingly similar construction, "走着瞧", has a different time structure, as the V2 is meant to be realized at a later time (Cf: "你等着瞧！" Chen 1986: 10).

(ii) Mangione has cited three examples from an 18th Century vernacular novel, 儒林外史, and one example from Sun (1979). However, everyone of these four examples has a comma punctuation immediately following the V1-zhe (NP). It should have been obvious to Mangione that this comma punctuation makes a whole world of difference: The sentences are of a different structure, hence are completely irrelevant to his argument. Punctuation marks cannot be taken slightly, much less ignored totally, in grammatical analysis of a sentence. The use of the commas in those sentences indeed shows that the authors felt that it would be wrong if the two verbs, thus stated, were not separated in some way. Those examples, therefore, confirm, rather than negate, the validity of my constraints.

Here, four out of seven presumed counterexamples have turned out to be irrelevant, as they are of a different structure. This shows carelessness.

3. Mangione states that "It should be noted that C (meaning Chen) gives no indication that the judgments reported in his paper are based on a representative sample." Being a native speaker myself, I was aware that such constructions are extremely rare, either in speech or in print. Nevertheless, I had double-checked with several native speakers and confirmed the judgments made in my paper. However, in this regard, I wish to point out to Mangione that linguists are not public poll surveyors; hence, random sampling is not always a necessary component in their works. When faced with obvious and confirmed inconsistencies, it is for the linguists to find out how and why rather than for the public to vote for or against, brushing aside the how and why.

4. Mangione was right, however, in admitting that his sample was small and unrepresentative. Since the report on native speakers' responses and the presumed counterexamples constituted the bulk of his note, a sample involving five subjects was much too small to be of any significance, especially when the weighting in the informants' responses showed no bias

either way. Actually, acceptability can never be a profitable line of argument. That was why both Chu's (1987) paper and mine (1987) focused on approaches and technicalities instead.

REFERENCES

CHEN, Chung-yu. 1986a. Constraints on the 'V1-zhe...V2' Structure. *Journal of Chinese Language Teachers Association* 21.1:1-20.

CHEN, Chung-yu. 1986b. On the Physical Modality of English Verbs. *Papers in Linguistics* (Canada) 19.2:131-54.

CHEN, Chung-yu. 1987. Stemming from the Verbal Suffix -zhe. *Journal of Chinese Language Teachers Association* 22.1:43-64.

CHEN, Qiufan (adapter). 1972. 濟公傳. 東方出版社. Taipei.

CHU, Chauncey C. 1987. The Semantics, Syntax and Pragmatics of the Verbal Suffix -Zhe. *Journal of Chinese Language Teachers Association* 22.1: 1-42.

MANGIONE, L. 1987. A Note on Some -Zhe Sentences. *Journal of Chinese Language Teachers Association* 22.1:69-86.

SUN, Li. 1979. *Cun Ge*. Renmin Wenxue Chubanshe. Beijing.

TIME STRUCTURE OF ENGLISH VERBS

Abstract.

The present work focuses on the feature [durative]. Attempts have been made to refine and extend Vendler's analysis. However, the contention here is that verbs should not be discussed in the context of superimposed qualifications (e.g. *to draw a circle*) or quantifications (e.g. *to run a mile*), for such an allowance of superimpositions is open-ended. The contrast in [± durative] is not only a necessary and sufficient distinction in the time structure of English verbs, but also the only distinction that can be made without adding superimpositions to the verbs. The perfect continuous aspect rather than the simple continuous, which Vendler uses, has been proved to be the valid frame for the testing of the time structure of verbs. The change of state for both achievements and accomplishments are proved to occur at a point in time rather than in an interval as claimed by Dowty.

1. Admissibility of the Simple Continuous Aspect as the Primary Criterion Distinguishing Verbal Classes in Vendler's Framework.

In his interesting discussion of time structure of verbs, Zeno Vendler (1967) considers admissibility of the simple continuous aspect as the primary criterion in distinguishing verbal classes. ('Continuous' and 'progressive' are used as synonyms in this paper.) In his framework, *states* and *achievements* are verbs lacking continuous aspects; *activities* and *accomplishments* are those which do admit continuous aspects. Such a criterion certainly needs revision, for it cannot account for some obvious discrepancies.

Love is one of his states. Yet, it may occur with a continuous aspect as in

(1a) Until the twelfth of never, I'll still be loving you. (- a popular song)

Die is one of his achievements, yet one can easily say

(2a) He is/was dying.

Vendler is, of course, aware of the fact that *die* is a momentary transition. However, as admissibility of continuous aspect is the primary demarcation in his framework, such apparent discrepancies are not to be taken for granted.

In fact, the unmarked continuous aspect (e.g., *he is playing*), as opposed to the marked perfect continuous (e.g., *he has been playing*), is not a valid frame for the testing of the time structure of verbs. It is the perfect continuous aspect that is the valid frame:

(1b) *He has been loving you for the last three years.

(2b) *He has been dying for the last three days.

For further illustration of this point, quite a few verbs of momentary transitions or actions occur with the unmarked continuous aspect, which then indicate immediate futurity or iteration rather than progress. *Leave (a place)*, for instance, is a categorical notion (as opposed to a scalar notion), for one is either at a certain place or not at that place. The fact that this verb does not admit the perfect continuous aspect, when referring to a single happening of the act of *leaving* (3), shows that *leave (a place)* denotes a momentary transition. That is, it would be an achievement term in Vendler's classification.

(3) *I've been leaving the U.S. for the last two days.

Not even when the person is on an airplane which took off ten minutes ago can he say

(4) *I've been leaving the U.S. for the last ten minutes.

But this verb can occur with the unmarked continuous aspect as in (5), which admits of futurate interpretation but not an imperfective interpretation.

(5) I'm leaving the U.S. (the day after tomorrow).

And it is this frequent use of the continuous aspect for futurity that has brought about the misconception that *leave (a place)* is a process rather than a transition.

One may argue that when a person says *John is leaving town*, John may be striding down the main street, or he may even be outside the town boundary. Therefore, *leave (a place)* is not a categorical notion and is a process rather than a point-transition.

To say *John is leaving town* when John is actually striding down the main street (i.e. still in town, has not left the town yet) is just like saying (*You'd better hurry,*) *he is dying* when the person is lying in bed in an intensive care unit (i.e. still alive, has not died yet). And to say *John is leaving town* when John has actually passed the town boundary is just like saying (*You'd better hurry,*) *he's dying* without knowing that at the moment of speaking, the person has already passed away in the hospital.

When John is striding down the main street or lying on a hospital bed, he is approaching a point-transition rather than undergoing a process. The fact that *leave (a place)* does not admit the perfect continuous aspect shows that this verb, like *die*, is an instantaneous transition (Cf. 3.1 *fall asleep*).

Thus, it has been proved that the unmarked continuous aspect cannot serve as a frame to distinguish between state verbs and action verbs or to test the time structure of action verbs; the perfect continuous aspect (especially when paired with an adverbial denoting a short span of time) is the right frame.

A [-durative] verb may acquire a [+durative] syntactic behavior (i.e., occurring in the perfect continuous aspect) through iteration. The action may be repeated by the same agent or patient (in certain case relation terminology, the grammatical subject of a sentence containing an intransitive verb is labeled a patient) or by different agents or patients.

(6) The younger generation have been leaving this town in great numbers.
(7a) Your little boy has been jumping and shouting for the whole morning.
(7b) A lot of people have been jumping from this cliff to their death since last summer.

Since the time structure of a verb is the time structure of a verb as denoting a single happening of an action, iterative progressives must be kept strictly apart from imperfective progressives, or many crucial aspectual distinctions between the verbs will be obscured. The difference between a genuine progressive, i.e. an imperfective progressive, and an iterative progressive of a [-durative] verb is comparable to the difference between a lengthened [m̩] sound and a series of rapidly repeated [pə] sounds. While it is possible to phonate both a lengthened syllabic [m̩] for 10 seconds and a rapid series of [pə] sounds for 10 seconds, the [m̩] sound is produced by a single act of articulation whereas the [pə] sounds are produced by a series of repeated articulations. [m̩] is [+durative] and [p] is still [-durative].

The formulation below characterizes the acquisition of a [+durative] syntactic behavior through iteration by a [-durative] verb:

$$([\text{-durative}])^{Pl} \rightarrow [+\text{durative}]/\text{surface}$$

2. Problems with Vendler's 'Accomplishments'.

Among verbs admitting continuous aspects, Vendler distinguishes between 'two important species': Verbs such as *running, pushing a cart*, etc., which do not have a 'set terminus', are activities. Verbs such as *running a mile, drawing a circle, writing a letter*, etc., which do have set terminus, are accomplishments.

There are, however, internal discrepancies among his accomplishment terms. For instance, while it is not possible to say

(8a) *He has been running a mile for the last 5 minutes,

it is perfectly legitimate to say

(9) He has been drawing a/that circle for the last 5 minutes.
(10) He has been writing a/that letter for the last 5 minutes.

Furthermore, Vendler maintains that if a runner has run a mile in four minutes, it cannot be true that he has run a mile in any period of that time. And similarly, if a person wrote a letter in an hour, he did not write it in the first quarter of that hour. Again, I find discrepancies in such an argument. It is true that if a person collapsed when he was doing his daily one-mile run, we cannot say

(11a) *He collapsed when he was running a mile.

Yet, we can say of a person who collapsed when writing a letter that

(12) He collapsed when he was writing a/that letter (or, drawing a /that circle).

What then is the source of these discrepancies among Vendler's 'accomplishments'? In my view, in the phrase *running a mile*, *a mile* is a quantification of running; whereas in the other two phrases, *a letter* and *a circle* are qualifications of *writing* and *drawing*, respectively. This difference explains the discrepancies shown in the aforementioned sentences.

Moreover, if we change the determiners in sentences (8a) and (11a), the two unacceptable sentences will become acceptable:

(8b) He has been running that/his mile for the last 5 minutes.
(11b) He collapsed while he was running that/his mile.

This is because *a mile* is a quantification of running, whereas *his mile* and *that mile* are qualifications of the running.

Such quanitifications or qualifications are indeed superimpositions on a verb rather than innate features of the verb. Such an allowance for superimpositions in the discussion of the time structure of verbs is an open-ended one. *Pushing a cart*, for example, is an activity in Vendler's discussion. But *pushing a cart to the other end of the street* would certainly be an accomplishment, for it proceeds toward a 'set terminus'. To say that the two phrases contain different species of verbs is certainly unconvincing. To provide another example, *drawing a circle* is an accomplishment. What about *drawing a tree*? Where is the 'set terminus'? *Eating an egg*, presumably, would be an accomplishment in Vendler's framework because, like *drawing a circle*, *eating an egg* proceeds toward a 'set terminus'. The phrase *eating omelet*, as it is, contains no apparent 'set terminus'. Shall we then say that one of the *eating's* is an accomplishment and the other is an activity?

In short, I find it unjustifiable to discuss the time structure of a verb in the context of superimposed qualifications or quantifications. The aspectual interpretation of a verb changes as various complements are added to the verb, and the linguist is led nowhere. It is my contention that in the discussion of the time structure of verbs, only the V's should be taken as a unit; VP's should not be a unit for consideration. Here a VP is defined as a *V + NP* structure (e.g., *pushing a cart, drawing a circle, running a mile*, etc.). A *V* can be either a 'bare verb' such as *push, draw, run, die*; etc. or a 'phrasal verb' such as *run out, die away, fall asleep, take off*, etc. Strictly speaking, as far as the time structure of a verb as a single lexical item denoting a single happening of an action is concerned, the contrast between [+durative] and [-durative] is not only a necessary and sufficient distinction, but is also the only distinction that can be made without adding superimpositions to the verb. ('A verb as a single lexical item' should not be taken as meaning a single 'word'. **Pushed** and ***was pushing***, for example, are different aspectual manifestations of the same single lexical item *push*, which is inherently [+durative].)

The notion of 'lexical item' (McCawley 1968) is vital in the discussion of the time structure of verbs. The verb *find*, for instance, which is obviously [-durative] in (13b), is a different lexical item from the *find* in (14), which is [+durative]. And the *find* in (15) meaning 'look for' is still another lexical item.

(13a) *I was finding a stranger sitting in my room.
(13b) I found a stranger sitting in my room.
(14) I'm finding him a bore.
(15) I was finding a book at the library when the fire alarm went off.

3. The Progressive Aspect.

3.1. Dowty's 'progressive analysis'.

Dowty has discussed verbs of accomplishments and achievements in terms of a 'progressive analysis'. In his discussion of 'imperfective progressives' and 'futurate progressives', there are, however, two points which seem to invite questions.

First, Dowty apparently has mistaken a case of futurate progressive for imperfective progressive. Consequently, he claims that the change of state for achievements occurs in an interval rather than a point in time. In my opinion, this is incorrect.

Dowty (1977: 40-50) equates the failure of inference from (16a, 17a) to (16b, 17b), which involve verbs of Vendler's achievement terms, to the failure of inference from (18a) to (18b), which involve a verb of Vendler's accomplishment terms.

    (16a)   John was falling asleep.
    (16b)   John fell asleep.

    (17a)   John was dying.
    (17b)   John died.

    (18a)   John was drawing a circle.
    (18b)   John drew a circle.

    (16c)   John was falling asleep when Mary shook him.
    (17c)   John was dying when the operation was performed which saved his life.

Citing two sentences (16c, 17c), he claims that for both accomplishments and achievements, the change of state occurs in an interval rather than at a point in time.

It is obvious that he has interpreted the progressive in (16a, c and 17a, c) as an imperfective progressive. But it is actually a futurate progressive, as can be proved by the fact that sentence (18a) can be transformed into perfect continuous, whereas (16a) and (17a) cannot be thus transformed.

    (18c)   John has been drawing that circle for the last ten minutes.
    (16d)   *John has been falling asleep for the last ten minutes.
    (17d)   *John has been dying for the last ten minutes/days.

The fact that *die* and *fall asleep* are incompatible with the perfect continuous aspect indicates that they are deictic notions. They denote transitions that are instantaneous. Just like in the case of *leave (a place)* (Cf. 1.), the frequent use of the unmarked continuous aspect for futurity has brought about the misconception that *fall asleep* is a process.

The perfect aspect in (16e and 17e) marks the completion of an instantaneous transition which gives rise to a static state of affairs as depicted by (16f and 17f).

    (16e)   John has fallen asleep.
    (16f)   John is asleep.

    (17e)   John has died.
    (17f)   John is dead.

Dowty has confused the futurate progressive with the imperfective progressive in his discussion of *die* and *fall asleep*. Consequently, his claim that the change of state for achievements (and accomplishments) occurs in an interval rather than at a point in time is not valid.

My contention is that the progressive in sentences (16a, 17a) is a futurate progressive, which is the only type of progressive compatible with achievement terms denoting single happenings of an action (Cf. Sections 1, and 3.2, for the difference between imperfective progressives and iterative progressives). And the patients in the two sentences were APPROACHING an instantaneous transition rather than UNDERGOING a transition. The change of state occurs at a point in time for achievement terms. The progressive in (18a, *he was drawing a circle*), where the verb is an accomplishment term, is an imperfective progressive. While the act of drawing occurs in a period of time (i.e. an interval), the two ends meet and form a circle at a point in time. Hence, the change of state for accomplishments also occurs at a point in time. This is comparable to the fact that while the process of saturation occurs in a period of time, the saturation point is reached at a point in time. Thus, for both achievements and accomplishments, the change of state occurs at a point in time.

3.2. A three-way contrast: futurate, imperfective, and iterative.

Concerning the progressive aspect my second submission is that Dowty makes a generalization in connection with the formal property of futurate progressive, which is an over-simplification of the reality. Here, there is a crucial point to be considered.

Dowty (1977:71) states that futurate progressives do not always have an explicit future time adverbial. The validity of this statement holds only with certain verbs, but not with others.

With verbs which have an innate aspectual characteristic [-durative], it is true that futurate progressives may or may not have an explicit time adverbial (19, 20).

(19) He is leaving town (tomorrow).
(20) The condemned men are dying (tomorrow).

This is because [-durative] verbs, when denoting single happenings of an action, are by definition incompatible with a genuine progressive, i.e. imperfective progressive. As stated in Section 1.1, even when a person is on an airplane which took off ten minutes ago, he still cannot say

(4) *I've been leaving the U.S. for the last ten minutes.

And the condemned men who are dying may be perfectly healthy and fit. Both the condemned men and the terminal cancer patients who are dying are approaching the transition, for one cause or another, rather than undergoing the transition. [-durative] verbs such as *die, fall asleep, leave (a place)*, etc. are strict point-transition verbs. Hence, the only possible aspectual interpretation of (19, 20), with or without a future time adverbial, is the futurate progressive.

When verbs which are [+durative] in nature occur in a simple progressive aspect in the absence of an explicit time adverbial, the sentences either are ambiguous, accommodating both the futurate and the imperfective (as well as the iterative) interpretations, or exhibit only the imperfective progressive. For instance, sentence (21a), which does not contain a future time adverbial, can be understood either as an imperfective progressive (i.e., depicting what is actually going on in the real world or on TV) or as a futurate progressive (i.e., the same as (21b)).

(21a) The Yankees are playing the Red Socks.
(21b) Tomorrow the Yankees are playing the Red Socks.

And sentence (22), which does not have a future time adverbial, is usually taken as an imperfective progressive, i.e., different from (23), which indicates futurity.

    (22)   I'm taking Elementary French.
    (23)   I'm taking Elementary French next year.

To sum up, a futurate progressive may or may not have an explicit time adverbial when the verb is [-durative] in nature, because the [-durative] characteristic does not permit an imperfective interpretation. In the case of [+durative] verbs, the absence of a future time adverbial will lead either to ambiguity (accommodating both futurate and imperfective interpretations) or to an imperfective interpretation, depending on the individual verbs. As stated earlier, the distinction between an imperfective progressive and an iterative progressive is crucial to a correct understanding of the aspectual characters of the verbs.

The discussion in this section aims at a clarification of a confusion between the imperfective and the futurate progressives as well as a confusion between the imperfective and the iterative progressives, and hence, a further explication of Vendler's achievement and accomplishment terms. Nevertheless, my position on the time structure of verbs still remains unchanged. That is, the contrast between [+durative] and [-durative] is not only a necessary and sufficient distinction, but also the only distinction that can be made without adding superimpositions to the verbs.

REFERENCES

CHEN, Chung-yu. (1978) Aspectual features of the verb and the relative positions of the locative. *Journal of Chinese Linguistics* 6.1:76-103.

COMRIE, Bernard. (1976) *Aspect*. Cambridge University Press.

DOWTY, David R. (1977) Towards a semantic analysis of verb aspect and the English 'imperfective' progressive. *Linguistics and Philosophy* 1:45-77.

LYONS, John (1977) *Semantics*. (Vol 1 & 2) Cambridge University Press.

MCCAWLEY, James D. (1968) The role of semantics in a grammar. *Universals in Linguistic Theory*. E. Bach and R. Harms, eds. Holt, Rinehart and Winston. 125-170.

VENDLER, Zeno. (1967) *Linguistics in Philosophy*. Cornell University Press.

WEINREICH, Uriel. (1966) Explorations in semantic theory. *Current Trends in Linguistics III*.

ON THE PHYSICAL MODALITY OF ENGLISH VERBS

Abstract.

The crucial difference between the syntactic minimal pair *John washes his car in the garage* and *John keeps his car in the garage* does not lie in the locatives, but in the physical modality of the two verbs. Three types of physical modality for action verbs are distinguished on the basis of corresponding syntactic behavior: [+active] (e.g. *wash*), [-active] (e.g. *keep*), and [+ → -active] (e.g. *put, hang, sit ;* verbs which contain in themselves both the [+active] inceptive motion and the subsequent [-active] static state of affairs). Two kinds of inceptions are recognized: WEAK INCEPTION is implicit in certain [-active] verbs (e.g. *leave (something)* as opposed to *keep*, which is [-inceptive]); STRONG INCEPTION gives rise to two types of transmutation of aspectual characters, [+ → -active] and [+ → -transitive] (e.g. *He hung her picture on the cupboard* as opposed to *Her picture is hanging on the cupboard*), which are changes that take place within a single happening of an action.

Vendler's concept of inception (as in *know, understand*) appears to be useless in grammatical analysis. Moreover, it seems that all the items under Vendler's "generic states" can be redistributed to other categories. In the discussion of physical modality of verbs, only those aspectual distinctions which are reflected in the formal linguistic expression should be taken into account.

1. **The Feature [active].**

1.1. **Inadequacies of time schemata as the sole parameter in the analysis of verbs.**

In Vendler's framework, "states" are characterized by the lack of continuous aspects. Verbs such as *rule, dominate*, etc. are "generic states" in his classification. While it is true that the king of Cambodia can hardly say that he *was ruling* Cambodia all morning (Vendler 1967:109; here only the grammatical structure is discussed, not the truth value), the following sentences in which these verbs occur in continuous aspects (particularly, perfect continuous) are perfectly legitimate:

(1a) Who is ruling the country now?
(1b) He has been ruling the country for the last 10 years.

(2a) One man was dominating the committee for the whole morning.
(2b) She has been dominating her husband ever since they got married.

These verbs, which Vendler labeled "generic states", not only admit the unmarked continuous aspect but also the perfect continuous aspect. This fact indicates that time schemata alone are seriously inadequate to account for the behavior of verbs with respect to the admission of different aspects. It is my position that the physical modalities or configurations of the action denoted also play a vital role (complementing the role of time schemata) in the account of the behavior of the verbs. I shall justify this position in the following discussion.

1.2. **Physical modality as a parameter.**

In this section I shall examine the relationship between the physical modality of the action denoted and the compatibilities of the verb with different aspects. Let me start with a famous problem in the literature.

(3)   John washes his car in the garage.
(4)   John keeps his car in the garage.

The syntactic minimal pair, (3) and (4), has been discussed in terms of the function of the locatives in the literature. Fillmore (1968: 26) envisages a difference in the case relations of the two locatives. He interprets the locative in (3) as an "outer locative", which in its selectional properties is similar to the benefective case. The restriction of this "outer locative" in the selection of verbs, according to Fillmore, may have more to do with dependency relations between cases than with dependencies directly connected with the verb. Tai (1975:176) sees a semantic distinction in the functions of the two locatives. He claims that while the locative in (3) denotes the location of the action *wash*, the locative in (4) denotes the location of the patient *his car*. I shall illustrate that such focuses on the locatives in the account of the essential difference between the two sentences are incorrect.

It is my view that in both sentences the place adverbial denotes the location of the action, i.e., modifies the verb. However, the realizations of the two actions denoted by the two verbs differ in their physical modalities or configurations. I shall substantiate this point in the following discussions.

1.2.1. [+active] vs [-active].

(5a)   John washed/painted his car in the garage.
(5b)   John kept/left his car in the garage.

What is common between the two sentences is that in both sentences *his car* was in the garage. What makes them different is that while John, the agent, was necessarily in the garage in (5a), he was not necessarily in the garage in (5b). In fact, there is a tendency to expect John not to be present in the garage with his car at the moment of speaking. This difference, as illustrated in (6a, 6b), has been generally acknowledged.

(6a)   *John washed/painted his car in the garage, but he himself

was not in the garage.
(6b)   John kept/left his car in the garage, but he himself was not in the garage.

A preliminary conclusion can now be drawn: The nature of verbs such as *wash, paint, polish, build*, etc. is such that during the course of the action they denote, the agent must be present; whereas with verbs such as *keep, leave (something)*, the agent's presence is not required. The next step is to search for an explanation.

Let us examine the roles of the patient *car* in the two sentences (5a, b). While the car in (5a) had to undergo a treatment (it was washed/painted), the car in (5b) was just being present there without being manipulated in any way. Nothing actually "happened" to it. This explains why the presence of the agent is not required.

While verbs such as *wash, paint, polish, build*, etc. are [+active] throughout the whole course of the action they denote, verbs such as *keep, leave (something)*, etc. are in reality [-active]. These verbs indeed denote the agent's "disposal" rather than his "manipulation" of the patient. Nothing physical happens. Granted that for every occurrence of *keeping, leaving (something)*, there must have been an active, inceptive motion, the physical inceptive motion is, nevertheless, not contained in the verb. I have two reasons for this claim, and I shall use sentence (7) to illustrate them.

(7)   John's car is kept/left in the garage.

In the first place, the tense in (7) is present, but the car is already in the garage and the physical inceptive motion by which John got his car into the garage took place in the past. Second, by looking at sentence (7) we have no way to tell how he got his car into the garage. Did he drive the car into it? Did he push it in? Or did he use a crane? The verbs *keep, leave* cannot provide any information on the actual inceptive motion because they do not contain in themselves the actual inceptive motion. As stated before, they express only the agent's "disposal" of the object. And the fact that John's car is in the garage for sentence (4) is a consequence of John's disposal of his car.

This difference in semantics is reflected in the syntactic behavior of the verbs as illustrated below.

A. Compatibilities with the simple aspect (i.e. noncontinuous, nonperfect) connoting progress:

(8a) At this moment, his car is being washed/painted in the garage.
(8b) At this moment, his car is washed/painted in the garage.

(9a) *At this moment, his car is washed/painted in the garage.
(9b) At this moment, his car is kept/left in the garage.

As manifested in the examples, with verbs such as *wash, paint*, etc., the simple aspect cannot connote an on-going process (9a). To connote what is in progress, employment of the continuous aspect is indispensable (8a). On the other hand, with verbs such as *keep, leave (something)*, etc., both the continuous aspect (8b) and the simple aspect (9b) may connote an existing fact. This is precisely because these verbs are intrinsically [-active] in their physical modality. I shall verify this point immediately:

Both sentences (8a) and (8b) are acceptable sentences. However, if we change the word order in them or delete the locative clause, one of them will become unacceptable (10b, 11b).

(10a) His car is being washed/painted.
(10b) *His car is being kept/left.

(11a) His car is in the garage being washed/painted.
(11b) *His car is in the garage being kept/left.

(11a) is acceptable and well-formed because "being washed/painted" constitutes a separate piece of information supplementing the information carried by the clause. (11b), on the other hand, is not acceptable because "being kept/left" is semantically inadequate to constitute a sound piece of information. As stated earlier, these verbs do not contain in themselves the actual inceptive motion. Therefore, they are seriously inadequate to be the information "focus" of a sentence (10b). Other information such as on the location, time, agent, patient, or manner, etc. are required to make the message complete.

This also explains the ungrammaticality of (12b) as opposed to (12a). ((12a, b) provided by McCawley, p.c.)

(12a) John washes his car in the garage, and Bill does so in the alley.
(12b) *John keeps his car in the garage, and Bill does so in the alley.

B. Compatibilities with the perfect continuous aspect paired with a short time span:

(13a) John has been washing/painting his car in the garage.
(13b) John has been keeping/leaving his car in the garage.

(14a) John has been washing/painting his car in the garage for the last 10 minutes.
(14b) *John has been keeping/leaving his car in the garage for the last 10 minutes. (Cf. Section 3)

The two types of verbs also differ in their relationship with the time adverbial. While both (13a) and (13b) are perfectly acceptable, (14b) gave my informants a difficult time. They were literally "uncomfortable". Finally they decided that it was grammatically correct, but they themselves would never say it. One informant said that 10 minutes was too short. But I suppose no one will feel uncomfortable about.

(15) I'll let you keep/leave your car in my garage for 10 minutes,

except perhaps wonder why the speaker should bother to be generous. Sentence (15) seems to indicate that time is irrelevant. But, as a matter of fact, it is not totally irrelevant. Sentence (16), in which the time span is not "too short", is quite acceptable.

(16)   He has been keeping/leaving his car in the garage for the last three weeks.

It seems that when a perfect continuous aspect is paired with a short time span as in the frame

(17)   He has been V-ing (NP) for the last 10 minutes,

we tend to expect that something "active" or "physical" is going on. That is, the person is actively engaged in doing something. And when the time span becomes long enough, the interpretation of an "active commitment" is automatically filtered out, and the interpretation of a "habitual activity" or a "constant or perpetual state" comes in. Sentence (14b) is, therefore, not semantically well-formed because the perfect continuous aspect together with a short time span anticipates an active commitment, yet *keep* and *leave (something)* are [-active] in nature. (Cf. Section 3.)

I believe this furnishes sufficient evidence, both semantic and structural, to demonstrate that verbs such as *keep* and *leave* are intrinsically [-active]. They denote a static state of affairs which is consequent upon an active inceptive motion. The active motion, nevertheless, is not contained in the verb itself.

I have illustrated my point that in both sentences (3) and (4) the place adverbials modify the verbs; the only difference lies between the two transitive verbs: while *wash* is [+active], *keep* is [-active]. I shall label the [+active] verbs MANIPULATION verbs, and the [-active] verbs DISPOSAL verbs. The syntactic behavior of the two types of verbs as manifested in the examples cited is summarized in Table (17a).

(17a)   Syntactic behavior of certain transitive action verbs (Cf. (9 a-b), (10a-b), (14a-b)).

Verb type	Physical modality	Connoting progress with the simple aspect	Compatible with the perfect continuous aspect and a short time span	Constituting a sound piece of information
Manipulation verbs (e.g. *wash*)	[+active]	−	+	+
Disposal verbs (e.g. *keep*)	[-active]	+	−	−

It has been proved that certain action verbs are indeed [-active] in their physical modality. Nevertheless, I would like to elaborate on the notion of [-active] action verbs (i.e. disposal verbs) with another verb of this category yet differing from *keep* and *leave* with respect to other features.

The verb *give*, for example, is another member of this category:

(18) His father gave him a beautiful house.

(19) His father gave him ten thousand dollars.

(20) We have already given him a warning.

Upon hearing sentence (18), one would not know whether the father bought a house for the son or signed away a house of his own. (19) does not tell us how the money was paid (in cash or in a check) or how it was delivered (handed over or transferred from a bank account to another). Similarly, (20) provides no information on the form in which the warning was issued. *Buy* is another verb of this category. In short, verbs such as *give, buy* do not contain a physical action in them. [-active] action verbs such as *keep, leave (something), give, buy*, etc. denote only the agent's disposal of a concrete or abstract entity without illucidating the physical action by which his disposal is materialized. The materialization of the disposal is based upon actions of various kinds.

As stated earlier, the verb *give* is used to illustrate the notion of [-active] action verbs and it differs from *keep* and *leave (something)* in respect to other features (such as [venue]). Therefore, the syntactic behavior of verbs like *keep* as described in (17a) does not apply to *give*.

1.2.2. [+active], [-active] vs [+ → -active].

Two kinds of physical modality and hence two types of transitive action verbs (the manipulation verbs and the disposal verbs) have been distinguished on the basis of their semantic denotations as well as the differences in their syntactic behavior.

There is, however, a group of transitive verbs which behave syntactically like both the manipulation verbs and the disposal verbs. Such verbs include *place, load*, etc. Examples are given below.

A. Compatibilities with the simple aspect connoting progress:

(21a) *At this moment, the cups are washed / cleaned in the dishwasher.
(21b) At this moment, the cups are kept/left in the dishwasher.
(21c) At this moment, the cups are place / loaded in the dishwasher.

B. Compatibilities with the perfect continuous aspect paired with a short time span:

(22a) He has been washing/cleaning the cups in the sink for the last 10 minutes.

(22b) *He has been keeping/leaving the cups in the sink for the last 10 minutes.
(22c) He has been placing the cups in the sink for the last 10 minutes. (Or,...loading...into...)

The fact that verbs such as *place* and *load* behave syntactically like both the disposal verbs and the manipulation verbs has its root in semantics. These verbs contain in themselves both the active inceptive motion and the consequential static state of affairs, which can be termed a "residue" of the active inception. In other words, these verbs denote an active phase of an action (i.e., the inception) followed by an inactive continuum (i.e., the residue) in reality. Such a physical modality can be characterized as [+ → -actve] (Cf. 2.2). Note that the [+ → -] notation signals a change of feature in temporal sequence, and it should not be misconstrued as [±].

Occurring in a simple aspect as in (21c), these verbs connote an inactive modality, i.e., the second phase of the action, the residue. Occurring in a continuous aspect as in (22c), these verbs connote an active modality, i.e., the first phase of the action, the actual inceptive motion (Cf. 2.2). Having contained in themselves the active inceptive phase, these verbs are semantically adequate to convey a sound piece of information, i.e., to constitute the information focus of the sentence (23c, 24).

(23a) The cups are in the kitchen being washed/cleaned in the dishwasher.
(23b) *The cups are in the kitchen being kept/left in the dishwasher.
(23c) The cups are in the kitchen being placed in the dishwasher. (Or,...loaded...into...)

I shall label these verbs MANIPULATION-DISPOSAL verbs, for they contain in themselves the two successive phases of the action. Table (17a) may now be expanded to (17b).

(17b)

Verb type	Physical modality	Connoting progress with the simple aspect	Compatible with the perfect continuous aspect and a short time span	Constituting a sound piece of information
Manipulation verbs (e.g. *wash*)	[+active]	−	+	+
Disposal verbs (e.g. *keep*)	[-active]	+	−	−
Manipulation-disposal verbs (e.g. *place*)	[+ → -active]	+	+	+

The feature [+ → -active] certainly is not limited to transitive verbs only. Intransitive motion verbs such as *sit, stand*, also contain the two successive phases, an active phase followed by an static phase (Cf. 2.2).

1.3. On Vendler's "generic states".

1.3.1. Verbs *rule* and *dominate*: [-active] action verbs.

Having discovered certain correlations between the syntactic behavior of a verb and the physical modality of the action denoted, I shall now examine the syntactic behavior of some of Vendler's "generic state" verbs so as to clarify their physical modality.

Syntactically, both *rule* and *dominate* admit the perfect continuous aspect, therefore, they are not state verbs but action verbs (25a-d, 26a-d):

(25a)   At this moment, the country is being ruled by a tyrant.
(25b)   At this moment, the country is ruled by a tyrant.
(25c)   *The tyrant has been ruling the country for the last 10 minutes.
(25d)   *The country is being ruled.

(26a)   At this moment, he is being dominated by his wife.
(26b)   At this moment, he is dominated by his wife.
(26c)   She has been dominating her husband (/the conversation) for the last 10 minutes.
(26d)   He is being dominated.

Even though there may be finer distinctions between *rule* and *dominate* (the latter seems to be more 'intense'), the syntactic behaviors of the two verbs clearly point to a [-active] modality. It is now evident that they are indeed disposal verbs just like *keep, give*, etc.

1.3.2. Phrasal verbs *think that, believe that, believe in*: ordinary state verbs.

Think that (in the sense of "be of the opinion that" as in (27)), *believe that, believe in*, which are also "generic states" in Vendler's framework, on the other hand, do not admit the perfect continuous aspect; they behave just like ordinary state verbs such as *love, know*, etc.

(27)   I think that Jones is a rascal.

Semantically, verbs of Vendler's "generic states" are said to be "based upon actions of various kinds". This is consonant with my characterization of the disposal verbs, i.e. [-active] action verbs: Precisely because such verbs (e.g. *keep, give, rule*, etc.) do not contain any physical actions, the materialization of the actions denoted is non-specific and can be multi-formed.

Vendler maintains that *think that* (as in (27)) is rather like *rule*, for its is materialization is also "based upon actions of various kinds". To this I disagree. A king can be doing nothing all day long and yet still rules the country; the ministers of various ministries are running the country under the king's orders or guidance. Thus, the materialization of *ruling* is "based upon actions of various kinds". On the other hand, *thinking that* (in the sense of "of the opinion that" as in (27)) cannot be materialized on the basis of "actions of various kinds". There might have been various facts or actions on the part of Jones that have led me to think that Jones is a rascal; that is, my opinion is formed on the basis of "John's actions of various kinds". But once the opinion has been formed, my thinking that way is not and cannot be "based upon" actions of various kinds in the way that the king's ruling of the country is "based upon" actions of various kinds. The two different modes of "based upon" must be differentiated. Besides, the singleness in the semantic denotation of *think that, believe that*, and *believe in* also contrasts with the non-specific and multi-formed semantic denotations of *rule* and *dominate*.

To sum up, among Vendler's generic states, *rule* and *dominate* are not state verbs, generic or otherwise; because they do admit the perfect continuous aspect. As their syntactic behaviors indicate, they are indeed [-active] action verbs. *Believe that, believe in, think that* (in the sense of "to be of the opinion that") are states just like *love, know*, etc. It seems that all the items under Vendler's category of "generic states" can be re-distributed to other categories.

2. The Notion of "Inception" and the Transmutation of Aspectual Character.

2.1. Vendler's concept of "inception".

Vendler makes a distinction between an achievement sense and a state sense in verbs such as *know, understand*, etc. He maintains that the *know* in sentences (28) and (29) is an achievement that initiates the state of *knowing* in (30).

    (28)   Now I know it!
    (29)   And then suddenly I knew!
    (30)   I know the answer.

However, I fail to see the significance in the distinction he makes, because for every state or activity there must have been an inception. Taken to its logical limit, every verb, be it a state term or an activity term, has such an "achievement" sense. This fact renders the claimed distinction null and void. Granted that this distinction relates importantly to other aspectual things in languages like Spanish, in English there is no corresponding formal distinction in the syntactic behavior of the two "senses" of the verb. I believe that in the discussion of English verbs, with respect to their time structure and physical modality, only those aspectual (and semantic) distinctions which are reflected in their formal, syntactic behavior should be taken into account.

Vendler (1967:111) also maintains that *think of something* very often seems to have an achievement sense, as in (31):

    (31)   Every time I see that picture, I think of you.

If we follow his argument as exemplified in (31), verbs such as *grin, eat* and, perhaps, all the other English verbs can also be marked as having such an achievement sense (32, 33). What, then, is the use of such a claim?

    (32)   Every time he sees a pretty girl, he grins.
    (33)   Every time I feel hungry, I eat some biscuit.

In short, Vendler's concept of inception is purely philosophical and bears no significance in grammatical analysis. In the following discussion, I shall deal with the notion of "inception" in terms of formal, linguistic manifestations.

2.2. Weak inception: [+inceptive] and strong inception: [+ (→ -) active].

Two types of inceptions are recognized in the present frame work, both are reflected in the formal, syntactic behavior of the verbs.

In the previous discussion, it has been proved that both *keep* and *leave (something)* are [-active] action verbs. However, while both sentences (34a, 34b) are acceptable, (35a) and (35b) are not equally grammatical.

(34a)   I'm leaving this book here for her.
(34b)   I'm keeping this book here for her.

(35a)   He left this book here for you at 3:30.
(35b)   *He kept this book here for you at 3:30.

This is because *leave (something)* is a [+inceptive] verb, and therefore compatible with a point in time; *keep*, on the other hand, is a [-inceptive] verb and is incompatible with a point in time (without utilizing another verb to signal the initiation). Thus, given the same situation, the two verbs are used differently with respect to tense:

(36a)   Where did you leave my book?
(36b)   Where do you keep my book?

While the distinction made here is between [+inceptive] and [-inceptive], I shall label this type of inception WEAK INCEPTION, for the inception is implicit in a [-active] verb.

Another type of inception recognized is labeled STRONG INCEPTION. This type of inception is exhibited in verbs which contains two different phases of physical modality, that is, verbs with the feature [+ → -active]. The existence of such a [+ → -active] transmutation of feature in transitive verbs such as *place, load* has already been proved through evidence in the syntactic behavior of these verbs (Cf. 1.2.2). In the following discussion, I shall concentrate on explicating the notion of strong inception.

Intransitive verbs *sit* and *stand* (motion), for instance, contain two different phases which are reflected in the time structure of the verbs. The first phase is an active inceptive motion which is [-durative], and hence does not admit the perfect continuous aspect. The second phase is a static continuum of the state of affairs at the termination of the inceptive motion. It is [+durative] (and [-active]) and hence admits the perfect continuous aspect.

(37a) I sat down (on the floor).
(37b) *I have been <u>sitting down</u> (on the floor) for a while.

(38a) I am sitting on the floor.
(38b) I have been sitting on the floor for a while.

It may be worth pointing out that sentence (37b') below is acceptable, because in it *down* is part of a place adverbial rather than a manner adverbial as in (37).

(37b') *I have been sitting <u>down on the floor</u> for a while.

When an adverbial phrase marking duration occurs with the simple aspect, the duration pertains to the second phase of the action, as the first phase is inherently [-durative]. E.g.,

(39) I sat there for 3 hours.
(40) He put the beer in the fridge for 3 hours.

An example of transitive verbs (other than *load, place* in 1.2.2) having such a [+ → -active] modality is *hang*. (41a) exhibits the active inceptive motion and (41b) and (41c) depict the static continuum of the state of affairs at the termination of the inceptive motion. Note the present tense in (41b-c) where the verb has entered into the [-active] phase.

(41a) He hung her picture on the cupboard.

(41b) Her picture is hung on the cupboard.
(41c) Her picture is hanging on the cupboard. (Cf. 2.3)

Strong inception should not be confused with causation. Causation involves both causality and agency (Lyons 1977), therefore is found only in transitive verbs. Strong inception is found in intransitive verbs as well (e.g. *sit*, etc.). Moreover, strong inception is an active inceptive motion whose terminal cross-section lasts. The active inception and the inactive continuum of the state of affairs at the termination of the inceptive motion together constitute one single happening of an action. Hence, my sitting on the floor now is a continuum of the terminal cross-section of an inceptive motion that took place ten minutes ago. Her picture's being on the cupboard now is a continuum of the terminal cross-section of his hanging it there two weeks ago. Such a "continuum of the terminal cross-section of an inceptive motion" is an on-going process. Hence, we can say

(38b) I have been sitting on the floor for a while.
(41d) Her picture has been hanging on the cupboard for two weeks.

Causation, on the other hand, involves two pieces of actions (or one action and one transition). When John killed Mary two weeks ago, Mary died two weeks ago. The killing was completed two weeks ago; her dying took place two weeks ago. Although we can say she is dead two weeks after her death; her death is not a "durative continuum" of his action *kill*. We can say

(38c) I am still sitting on the floor.

(41e) Her picture is still hanging on the cupboard.

because sitting and hanging are on-going processes. 'Death' is not an on-going process, thus we cannot say she is still dying two weeks after he killed her.

In short, causation involves two separate actions (or an action and a transition), whereas strong inception pertains to the first part of two successive phases of one single happening of an action that can be characterized as [+ → -active] in its physical modality.

2.3. The feature [+ → -transitive].

It has been illustrated that strong inception is virtually the first part of two clear-cut phases (active vs static) which take place in temporal sequence during the course of one single happening of an action. (See Chen 1978 for discussions on two-phase verbs in Chinese.) Furthermore, the cleavage of the two phases gives rise to a transmutation of feature in the form of [+ → -active]. In addition to this, the transition also triggers a transmutation in the feature [transitive] in certain verbs.

In the case of a strong inception in transitive verbs, the two phases of the action focus on different parties: the active inceptive motion focuses on the agent (42a, a'), the resultant static phase focuses on the patient (42b).

(42a)   He is/was hanging her picture on the cupboard.
(42a') He hung her picture on the cupboard.
(42b)   Her picture is/was hanging on the cupboard.

Unlike sentences (41a, b), where a change from the active voice to the passive voice has been involved, (42a) and (42b) exhibit the same active voice in a continuous aspect. How can the difference between (42a) and (42b) be accounted for? It can not be explained away as a case involving merely a grammatical transformation as in (43a, b).

(43a)   He is/was washing his car.
(43b)   His car is/was being washed.

Nor can it be dismissed as a case involving two different lexical items sharing the same phonological shape as in (44a, b).

(44a)   I'm seeing a patient now.

(44b)　I'm seeing double vision now.

What is involved between (42a) and (42b) is another case of transmutation of aspectual character. The verb *hang* has undergone a [+ → -transitive] transmutation in (42a, b). Such transmutation of the characteristics [active] and [transitive] occur only with certain venue-oriented verbs. Parallel phenomena also exist in Mandarin Chinese (Chen 1978).

Sentences (45a-c) summarize the discussion on such transmutations of aspectual characters.

(45a)　He hung her picture on the cupboard.
(45b)　Her picture is hung on the cupboard.
(45c)　Her picture is hanging on the cupboard.

Hang in (41a): [+active], [+transitive]
(41b): [-active], [+transitive]
(41c): [-active], [-transitive]

3.　Mutation of Aspectual Character and the Parameter "Context" (or "Situation").

(14b)　*John has been keeping his car in the garage for the last 10 minutes.

If John left his car in the garage ten minutes ago and is now on his way to the airport to take a plane to Hawaii for a vacation, sentence (14b) is unacceptable. However, given a deliberate context, (14b) can become acceptable. For instance, in a competition where people have to sneak their cars into a garage and keep them there undetected for as long as possible. The *keeping one's car in the garage* in this special context of a competition exhibits a physical modality which is different from that of the ordinary keeping one's car in the garage when it is not used. While the latter (i.e. the ordinary situation) expresses an inactive and inattentive dynamic continuum of a situation.

As stated earlier, the physical modality of a verb pertains to the physical configuration of the action denoted. When the action is materialized in a different way in a different situation, the physical modality and, hence, the syntactic behavior of the verb change accordingly. In the real world, any action may be materialized in many different ways. When the linguists characterize a verb with respect to its physical modality, they characterize it according to the most common way in which the action denoted is materialized. Hence, provisions must be made to account for the unusual/deviant ways of materialization of the action under unusual/deviant circumstances. Therefore, a provision in terms of "context" should be recognized as a necessary theoretical working parameter. Such change of the aspectual character of a verb when it occurs in a deviant context, or, rather, when the action denoted occurs in a deviant situation, can be referred to as 'mutation' of aspectual characters.

Transmutation of aspectual character (e.g. $[+ \rightarrow -\text{active}]$, $[+ \rightarrow -\text{transitive}]$) as discussed in the previous sections occur between two successive phases which take place in temporal sequence within a single happening of an action. Mutation of aspectual characters, on the other hand, refers to independent and sporadic changes in the characterization of the verb arising from a deviant materialization of the action denoted in a deviant situation.

4. Conclusion.

Verbs such as *keep, leave (something), rule, give, buy,* etc. are found to denote the agent's disposal of an entity without illucidating the physical action by which his disposal is materialized. In other words, they are [-active] action verbs, as opposed to the [+active] action verbs such as *wash, paint, build,* etc., which denote the agent's 'manipulation' of the patient.

There are verbs which contain in themselves an active inceptive motion and a subsequent static state of affairs. Such verbs include *sit, stand* motion and a subsequent static state of affairs. Such verbs include *sit, stand* (motion), *place, load, hang,* etc., and their physical modality can be characterized as [+ → -active]. With transitive verbs, the [+ → -active] modality triggers the change of [+ → -transitive]. The sentences below illustrate this point:

(41a) He hung her picture on the cupboard.
(41b) Her picture is hung on the cupboard.
(41c) Her picture is hanging on the cupboard.

Hang in (41a): [+active], [+transitive]
(41b): [-active], [+transitive]
(41c): [-active], [-transitive]

Two kinds of inceptions are distinguished: Weak inception is implicit in certain [-active] action verbs (e.g. *leave (something)* as opposed to *keep*). Strong inception refers to the active inceptive motion in the [+ → -active] verbs. Strong inception is different from causation.

I refer to the changes in [+ → -active] and [+ → -transitive] as "transmutation" in the aspectual characterization of verbs, as they each involve two linear phases which take place in temporal sequence within a single happening of an action.

Since the physical modality of a verb pertains to the physical configuration of the action denoted, when the action is materialized in a deviant manner under a deviant situation, the physical modality and, hence, the syntactic behavior of the verb change accordingly. To make provision for the fact that in the real world an action may sometimes be materialized in a deviant (i.e. unusual) manner, I refer to such deviant aspectual characterization of verbs as 'mutation' in the aspectual character of verbs and I propose a parameter 'context' for syntactic analysis.

Vendler's concept of inception (as in *know, understand*) appears to be useless in grammatical analysis. Moreover, it seems that all the items under Vendler's "generic states" can be redistributed to other categories.

are states just like *love* and know. In the discussion of the physical modality of verbs, only those aspectual distinctions which are reflected in the formal linguistic expression should be taken into account, for where the syntactic behavior of the verb and the aspectual characterizations of the action denoted correlate is where syntax and semantics fuse.

REFERENCES

CHAFE, Wallace L. (1970) *Meaning and the Structure of Language*. University of Chicago Press.

CHEN, Chung-yu. (1978) Aspectual features of the verb and the relative positions of the locative. *Journal of Chinese Linguistics* 6.1: 76-103.

CHEN, Chung-yu. (1982) On the time structure of English verbs. *Journal of Linguistics* 15.3: 181-90.

FILLMORE, Charles L. (1968) The case for case. *Universals in Linguistic Theory* E. Bach and R. Harms, eds. Hold, Rinehart and Winston. Pp. 1-88.

LYONS, John. (1977) *Semantics*. (Vol. 1 & 2) Cambridge University Press.

MCCAWLEY, James D. (1968) The role of semantics in a grammar. *Universals in Linguistic Theory*. E. Bach and R. Harms, eds. Holt, Rinehart and Winston. Pp. 125-70.

TAI, James. (1975) On two functions of place adverbials in Mandarin Chinese. *Journal of Chinese Liguistics* 3.2/3: 154-79.

VENDLER, Zeno. (1967) *Linguistics in Philosophy*. Cornell University Press.

WEINREICH, Uriel. (1966) Explorations in semantic theory. *Current Trends in Linguistics III*.

DYNAMISM IN THE ENGLISH STATIVE VERBS

Abstract.

Put under scrutiny here is the widely acknowledged distinction between STATES and DYNAMIC SITUATIONS. A distinction is made between DYNAMIC (i.e. potent or viable) and ACTIVE (i.e. motional). All English verbs are reckoned to be [+dynamic] in modality. It is under the feature of [+dynamic] that comes the division of + or - [active]. Verbs which have hitherto been regarded as states, e.g. *love, see, think, understand, know, stand, live*, etc., have a modality that can be characterized as [+dynamic, -active]. An aspectual feature [intense], which concerns the mode of realization of [-active] verbs and hence explains their relative admissibility into the progressive aspect is identified here. The stative verbs in Chinese, which are reckoned as adjectives by the laymen or some grammarians, are the ones which are genuinely [-dynamic] in modality.

0. Introduction.

It is a generally acknowledged view that the primary dichotomy on the aspectual character of English verbs falls between STATES and DYNAMIC SITUATIONS and that the principal distinguishing criterion is the admissibility of the progressive aspect (e.g. Vendler 1967; Quirk et al. 1972; Comrie 1976; Lyons 1977). However, this widely accepted framework has given rise to an amount of discrepancies that well exceeds any tolerable limit. For instance, Quirk et al. (1972:39) first provide the two categories with explicit and clear-cut definitions: 'When verbs (either habitually or in certain uses) will not admit the progressive, they are called STATIVE. When they will admit it, they are called DYNAMIC.' Yet they immediately make a compromise of the situation by saying that 'verbs that are almost always stative can usually be given a dynamic use on occasion'. Strictly speaking, such a proviso constitutes a flat contradiction to the definitions which they have stated in no uncertain terms and, thus, renders the distinction null and void.

This paper sets out to examine the nature of the inconsistencies and, subsequently, the validity of the dichotomy, and, in the meantime, search for possible missing distinction(s) that may be of vital importance in the discussion of verbal aspects.

1. Discrepancies in the Syntactic Characterization of States and the Inadequacies of Previous Treatments.

States have been qualified as incompatible with the progressive aspect as well as the imperative mood. Yet counterexamples are everywhere in evidence. Previous treatments are actually by-pass devices rather than solutions which offer explication to the apparent contradictions. In this connection, a few words on the inadequacies of the simple progressive aspect as the test frame are worth mentioning.

Vendler (1967), Comrie (1976), and Quirk et al. (1972) etc. have used the simple progressive aspect as a test frame to distinguish between states and dynamic situations. I (Chen 1982:182) have argued that the simple progressive aspect is not valid for the purpose; it is the perfect progressive that is a more reliable test frame, e.g.

(1a)　Until the twelfth of never, I'll still be loving you. (-- a popular song)
(1b)　*He has been loving you for the last three years.

(2a)　He is dying.

(2b)   *He has been dying for the last three days.

The following discussion, nevertheless, pertains to the interpretation of the discrepancies in earlier treatments rather than the validity of the test frames.

1.1. By-passing the problems through class labeling.

Quirk et al (1972:96) assert that 'the same verbs with other uses belong of course to other classes'. Hence, *smell* in (3a) is said to be a stative verb which indicates inert perception, and *smell* in (3b) is said to be a dynamic verb which indicates an activity.

(3a)   I (can) smell perfume   (Stative -- Quirk et al.)
(3b)   I am smelling perfume. (Dynamic -- Quirk et al.)

Similarly, Comrie (1976:36-37) talks about the 'non-stative use of stative verbs' in reference to the progressive form of the stative verb *understand* ('stative' by Vendler and Quirk et al. as well) as in

(4)   I am understanding more and more about quantum mathematics as each day goes by. (Non-stative use of a stative verb -- Comrie)

In those cases, a crucial theoretical defect has been lightly dismissed by a way of labeling which not only explains nothing but also leads to circularity. Hence, such treatments can be termed as a 'by-pass through class labeling'.

To maintain that it would be more accurate to speak of 'stative and dynamic uses of verbs' instead of 'stative and dynamic verbs', as do Quirk et al. (1972:94), offers no consolation either.

1.2. By-passing the problems through meaning interpretation.

Another type of treatment which has been employed by the linguists can be termed as a 'by-pass through meaning interpretation'.

Quirk et al. (1972:95) interpret the progressive forms of *be* and *have* as denoting different meanings:

(5a)   John has a car.   ('possesses')
(5b)   John is having a good time.   ('is experiencing')

(6a)   Mary is a good girl.   ('is by nature a good girl')
(6b)   Mary is being a good girl today.   ('is behaving well')

Such division of meanings not only is purely ad hoc but also unjustifiable. For instance, sentence (6a) can also be glossed as 'always behaves well'. Similarly, can there be two kinds of *love* in (1c) vs (1a), and (1d) vs (1e)?

(1c)   I love you.
(1a)   Until the twelfth of never, I'll still be loving you.   (-- a popular song)
(1d)   I love surfing.
(1e)   I went surfing yesterday, and I was loving every minute of it.

Comrie (1976:35) interprets the *seeing* in (7a) as used 'in the sense that I am only imagining things, in fact, there are no pink elephants for me to see'.

(7a)   I've only had six whiskies and already I'm seeing pink elephants.   ('am imagining')

The speaker of sentence (7a) might have been sober enough to talk about his tipsy condition with a little exaggeration. Or, it is equally probable that he was drunk enough to see pink elephants. A person under the effect of alcohol or drugs may hallucinate. And this hallucination is real to him. But sober or drunk, the speaker intended to say that he was experiencing the process of seeing pink elephants.

Likewise, a person who has just accidentally hit his head against a beam or a person suffering from certain problems in the eyes may utter sentences (7b) and (7c), respectively:

(7b) Oh, I'm seeing stars. Help me to a chair, quick!
(7c) I've been seeing sunspots since yesterday.

Linguists cannot take the liberty to interpret reported perception as mere imagination or to rectify the intended meaning of the speaker. Hence, the use of the progressive aspect in Comrie's sentence (7a) denotes precisely the PROCESS of *seeing* as PERCEIVING. Even for (7d) below, the linguists have no basis to declare that the speaker was not meaning perceiving.

(7d) Both Japan and Germany are seeing their overall trade surpluses continue to widen in dollar terms.

Another verb of inert perception, *hear*, a 'state' by Quirk et al. (1972: 96), can also occur in the progressive form to denote an on-going process:

(8a) I have been hearing buzzing sounds since yesterday morning.
(8b) I have been hearing incessant high-pitched noises ever since I recovered from that cold.

Chosen from Quirk et al.'s (1972:96) list of 'stative verbs of cognition', more examples can be added:

(9) I am knowing more and more about this person.

(10) You have been imagining things, my dear.

(11) We have been thinking of closing down that branch office.

(12) For years I have been guessing your intention.

(13) I was intending to tell you about it when you asked me.

And to choose from the 'relational stative verbs' listed by Quirk et al.

(1972:96), which are said to be usually impossible in the progressive aspect, there are these possible utterances:

(14) This jar <u>has been containing</u> water for a long time, therefore mosquitoes are breeding in it.

(15) He <u>has been depending</u> on me to supply the materials.

(16) This matter <u>has been concerning</u> me alone in the past, but now it concerns you as well.

(17) All along you <u>have been deserving</u> much more than this.

It should be clear that admissibility of the progressive aspect is a seriously defective criterion to distinguish between states and dynamic situations, as contrary sentences are everywhere in evidence.

1.3. Inadequacy of admissibility of the imperative mood as a demarcating criterion -- counterexamples.

Another syntactic criterion secondary to the admissibility of the progressive aspect is the admissibility of the imperative aspect (Quirk et al. 1972:402). The inadequacy, if not invalidity indeed, of this criterion is even more evident.

The verbs in the following counterexamples are taken from Quirk et al.'s lists of stative verbs (1972:96).

(18a) Love (Forgive/Believe/Depend on) me!
(18b) Taste (Smell) it!
(18c) Include me in!
(18d) Be good!
(18e) Guess who's coming to dinner!
(18f) Remember to post that letter!
(18g) Think harder!
(18h) See for yourself!

(18i)   Imagine finding yourself alone in an abandoned ship!
(18j)   Wish me luck!
(18k)   Hear me out!

2. Discrepancies in the Semantic Characterization of States.

The two syntactic criteria discussed above have failed in distinguishing between states and dynamic situations. The alternative, the semantic criteria, should also be subject to scrutiny.

2.1. The notion of 'no effort/energy' and the subsequent 'lastingness' of states.

Comrie (1976:49) maintains that to remain in a state requires no effort, whereas to remain in a dynamic situation does require effort, whether from inside or from outside. He also asserts, 'With a state, unless something happens to change that state, then the state will continue; this applies equally to *standing* and *knowing*.' A dynamic situation, on the other hand, will only continue if it is continuously subject to a new input of energy. Therefore, if John stops putting any energy into running, he will come to a stop.

While the above characterizations appear to be clear enough, there are state verbs which cannot fit into the description. Comrie (1976:37) maintains that *stand* (and presumably *sit* too) in the sense of being in a certain position, rather than of assuming a position, is a state. I should think that even in that sense, both *stand* and *sit* require continuous input of energy, as manifested by (19a) and (19b):

(19a)   I was exhausted after standing/sitting there for an hour; eventually I collapsed before the ceremony came to an end.
(19b)   I can't remain sitting up any longer, let me lie down.

Standing, sitting and *living* (also a state by Lyons 1977:706; Quirk et al. 1972:308) may discontinue without something happening to change them.

A person who is fit and fresh can remain standing for a reasonably long while until he decides to sit down or walk away. However, a person who is physically feeble is likely to collapse any moment after standing or sitting for some time. And if this person collapses while standing or sitting, it is not because something has happened to change that condition; rather, it is caused by the discontinuation of standing or sitting itself, owing to lack of sustaining effort/energy from within (cf. (19a)).

Put another way, it is the discontinuation of standing or sitting that has brought about the collapse, rather than the collapse changing the state of standing or sitting. This is comparable to the fact that when a heart patient dies, it is the stop of the heartbeat that brings about death, rather than death causes the heartbeat to stop.

To sum up, *stand*, *sit* and *live*, which have been classified as states, do require effort to continue and they may discontinue in the absence of an imposed change.

Verbs such as *think* and *imagine* are classified as states by Quirk et al. (1972:96), yet, they also require energy or effort. E.g.,

(20)   I'm too tired to think; ask me tomorrow.

Knowing, another verb which Comrie (1976:49) has put forward on this account, may also discontinue in the absence of an imposed change. Our knowledge of an event or a language learned in childhood may gradually wear thin and ultimately fall into oblivion without anything happening to change it. Here again it is not forgetting that changes the knowing; it is the discontinuation of knowing that gives rise to 'forgetting'.

2.2. The assumed homogeneity of states.

Lyons (1977: 483, 707) characterizes states as being homogeneous, continuous and unchanging throughout the period of their existence. The verb *understand* has been classified as a state by Comrie, Vendler and Quirk et al, yet Comrie (1976: 36-7) maintains that it can also refer to a developing process whose individual phases are essentially different from one another, as in

(4) I <u>am understanding</u> more and more about quantum mathematics as each day goes by.

Actually *understand* is a bona fide developing and, hence, changing process. Comrie's claim that this verb denotes a homogeneous and unchanging state yet 'can also refer to a developing process' actually contains a flat contradiction.

Love, a typical state term, affords a even more lucid explication, as it changes not only in quantity but also in quality:

(21a) I don't love him the way I used to any more.
(21b) I used to love her as a little sister, but now I love her as a woman.
(21c) My love for you will never change.

The classical pledge between lovers as given in (21c) is itself a revelation that love is typically subject to change. Mental activities such as *think* and *imagine* are actually processes of changes.

To sum up, on the demarcation between states and dynamic situations, not only are the syntactic criteria found to be invalid, but the semantic characterizations also turn out to be futile.

3. Probing into the Physical Modalities of States and Dynamic Situations.

3.1. Searching for possible submerged distinction(s) between motions and states.

Dynamic situations and states are generally distinguished as containing or not containing motions. For instance, Quirk et al. (1972:308) speak of 'MOTIONAL meaning' for verbs such as *go, move, fly* and 'STATIVE meaning' for verbs such as *be, stand, live*, which denote 'simple positions' or 'static locations'.

Such a conceptual framework has given rise to a number of paradoxical labelings. For example, Vendler (1967:109) qualifies certain action verbs (e.g. *rule, dominate*) as 'generic states'; the present author (Chen 1986, 1987) has talked about '[-active] action verbs' (e.g. *keep, leave (sth), rule, dominate, give,* etc.) and 'quasi-active verbs' in Chinese (e.g.<u>zhu</u> 'live', <u>deng</u> 'wait', <u>shui</u> 'sleep', <u>zhan</u> 'stand', which may occur with both the preverbal and the postverbal locatives involving <u>zai</u>). Such labelings reveal inadequacy in the MOTIONAL:STATIC dichotomy. This in turn suggests inaccuracy in the identification of the parameter used.

The motional: static dichotomy also brings about confusion in the classification of verbs of inert perception. Take the verb *see* as an example, as quoted in Vendler (1967:113), G. Ryle (1949) maintains that *seeing* is a kind of achievement; N. Sibley (1955) says, with apparent reservation, that *seeing* may turn out to be an activity. Vendler himself first claims (1967: 115) that *seeing* is not a process but a state or achievement, but later talks (1967:117) about the 'spontaneous activity of *seeing*'. Thus, he has actually adopted three options. Comrie (1976:35) feels that it is possible to view *seeing* and *hearing* either as states or as dynamic situations because different psychological theories differ as to just how ACTIVE a process perception is.

On the other hand, Comrie (1976:49) also maintains that the emission of sound from an oscilloscope is a dynamic situation because it requires continuous input of energy from its source of power. By the same token, the emission of light from a bulb should also be considered a dynamic situation because it too requires continuous input of energy from its source of power. The same question for perception verbs can be asked here: How ACTIVE a process is the emission of sound or light?

The emission of sound, classified by Comrie as being dynamic, is nevertheless, not motional. Now it is clear that there are two interpretations of dynamism or activeness at work.

The dynamism or activeness exemplified in the emission of sound (or light) or in the processes of *seeing* and *hearing* pertains to POTENCY and VIABILITY, which may or may not involve physical motions. On the other hand, the dynamism or activeness in *running, jumping, painting,* pertains essentially to physical motions. As a matter of fact, the two different senses are inherent in the word 'active', as exemplified by its uses as in (a) 'active sports' and (b) 'active ingredients' or 'a (radio-)active deposit'.

As revealed by their classifications, the aforementioned linguists (Vendler, Lyons, Quirk et al., etc.) have to date acknowledged only one type /sense of dynamism or activeness, namely that of physical motions. They have disregarded the other type/sense of activeness. Overlooking this subtle distinction, they classified many of the dynamic (in its second sense as given above) situations as states, and thereby gave rise to contrary sentences in terms of their supposed incompatibility with the progressive aspect as well as the imperative mood.

Comrie, who has recognized the dynamism in the emission of sound from an oscilloscope, nevertheless, has not proceeded to look into the grayish area or search for a possible missing link in the motional vs static dichotomy.

3.2. Identifying the submerged distinction: [+dynamic, --(physically) active].

For an accurate understanding of the aspectual characters of the verbs and, subsequently, a more realistic description or prescription of their syntactic behavior, the latter type of dynamism discussed above must be given due recognition. Hence, I propose to make a distinction between the two terms, 'DYNAMIC' and 'ACTIVE', which have to date been regarded as synonymous, and endow them with different meanings to meet the two different senses.

'Dynamic' is to be understood as POTENT, VIABLE; it may or may not be motional. 'Active' is to be understood as MOTIONAL, either physically or logically (e.g. *grow, change,* etc.) defined. Hence, what is dynamic may or may not be active; it is under the category of [+dynamic] that comes the division of [+active] and [-active]. Thus, the primary demarcation in English verbal aspect actually lies between [+dynamic, -active] and [+dynamic, +active], rather than the previously assumed [+dynamic/active] and [-dynamic/active].

The 'states vs dynamic situations' distinction in the previous works, as such, categorically precludes the recognition of states as being dynamic. However, the word 'state' itself by no means precludes a dynamic interpretation. This is evident in the following usages of the word:

(22a) a chronic inflammatory state
(22b) a continual state of disturbance
(22c) a turbulent state
(22d) an excited state of mind
(22e) an advanced state of decomposition
(22f) in a transition state
(22g) in the waking/sleeping state
(22h) in a dying state
(22i) in a state of unstable equilibrium
(22j) The ship was in a sinking state.
(22k) The country is in an unsettled state.

The above uses of the word STATE should serve to confirm that states are not necessarily static situations; they may very well be dynamic. In other words, what is static may still be dynamic (but not active, i.e. motional); examples of such verbs are **stand, sound, shine,** etc.

To sum up, what is static may still be dynamic. The state verbs of the previous works are here reckoned as having a dynamic modality, even though they are not motional. This much having been said, a logical conclusion is that all English verbs are [+dynamic] in modality. This [+dynamic, -active] modality explains the compatibility between state verbs and the progressive aspect. This compatibility, nevertheless, may be recessive in varying degrees for different verbs (Cf. Section 4).

4. The Feature [intense] in the [-active] Verbs.

The present analysis recognizes a distinction between [+dynamic, +active] and [+dynamic, -active], whereby DYNAMIC is to be understood as potent and viable; and ACTIVE is to be understood as motional. Since all English verbs have a [+dynamic] modality; they are all compatible with the progressive aspect (Cf. Section 2). (It is the imperfective progressive, rather than the futurate or iterative progressive that is the concern here.) However, while some [-active] verbs may denote an on-going process without utilizing the progressive aspect (e.g. *live*), others cannot do so (e.g. *wait*) (Chen 1986). Other parameters must have also been operating, which are responsible for this difference in their syntactic behavior.

One such parameter that has been discovered is the feature [intense], which is defined as a reference to the intensity of the potency or viability in the realization of an [-active] verb. Furthermore, while feature [active] is an absolute value to the verbs; [intense] appears to be a relative and gradient value, as it may change according to the modes of the realization (Cf. Section 4.2). The following discussion shall explore this feature through contrasting pairs of verbs, or different usages of the same verbs.

4.1. Discussion on *wait* (usually [+intense]) and *live* (usually [-intense]).

Both *wait* and *live* are verbs of unspecified materialization (Chen 1986), as they do not contain any specific physical actions in them. For instance, while waiting for John to ring me, I can be doing anything or nothing. And, needless to say, the living mortals may do all kinds of things or virtually nothing at different times through their lives. Hence, they are both [-active] (yet [+dynamic]) in modality. Nevertheless, there are differences in their syntactic behaviors. E.g., in denoting an on-going process, *wait* and *live* behave differently:

(23a) I live in New York.
(23b) I am living in New York.

(24a)   *I <u>wait</u> for you.
(24b)   I <u>am waiting</u> for you.

(24c)   ?She <u>has waited</u> eagerly for him to call since 9:00 a.m., and she's not giving it up.
(24d)   She <u>has been waiting</u> eagerly for him to call since 9:00 a.m., and she's not giving it up.

A comparison between the syntactic behavior of *live* and *wait* reveals that there may be some other features that are responsible for the well-formedness of sentence (23a) and the ungrammaticality of (24a) and, perhaps, in (24c) as well. It is reckoned here that the pertinent feature responsible for the difference between *wait* and *live* is [intense]. The singleness of goal or purpose in waiting makes it a much more intense process compared with that of living, which usually has much more diversified, if not indeed obscure, goals or purposes. As a [-intense] state of affairs, *live* may denote an on-going process without utilizing the progressive aspect (as in sentence 23a). whereas *wait*, which is [+intense] in its usual mode of realization, would require the progressive aspect to denote an on-going process (24b as opposed to 24a).

As stated above, the feature [intense] is a relative value as well as a variable; it may change according to the mode of the actual realization of the verb.

Under special circumstances, *live* may be materialized in an 'intense' manner. In such cases, *live* ([+intense]) cannot appear with the simple perfective to denote an on-going process; but must occur with the perfect progressive. E.g. (25b), as opposed to (25a) and (23a):

(25a)   *Ever since the doctor told him that he had only six months to live, he <u>has seized</u> life with both hands and <u>lived</u> every minute of it.
(25b)   Ever since the doctor told him that he had only six months to live, he <u>has been seizing</u> life with both hands and <u>living</u>

every minute of it.

On the other hand, *wait*, which is much more intense a process than *live*, may become [-intense] when the process of waiting has lasted long enough. In that case, the intensity has worn thin and the verb may appear in the simple perfect aspect to denote an on-going process as in (24e):

(24e) I have waited for him since Monday.
(24f) I have been waiting for him since Monday.

To sum up, the difference in the aspectual characters of *wait* and *live* pertains to the degrees of INTENSITY in the nature of the two events. *Live* is generally [-intense], but may become [+intense] when the mode of its realization is changed from the ordinary to the extraordinary (25b); *wait*, which is usually a much more intense process than live, may lose its intensity when the process has dragged long enough and the intensity has loosened up, hence the verb becomes compatible with the simple perfect aspect to denote an on-going process (e.g. 24e).

4.2. Discussion on *watch* (usually [+intense]) and *see* (usually [-intense]).

In the previous works, *see* has by and large been classified a state verbs (Quirk et al. 1972:96) and *watch*, a dynamic situation ('an active term' by Vendler 1967:113-120).

In the present analysis, both *see* and *watch* are reckoned to be [+dynamic, -active] in modality, because they both denote perception and involve the same amount of necessary physical movement. In fact, both can be materialized with no movement of the eyeballs or other parts of the body, accidentally incurred movements disregarded.

However, they differ in degrees of concentration on the part of the agent. *Watching* is purposeful and is therefore [+intense]; *seeing*, in its basic sense of visual perception, is a fortuitous event with respect to the objects that come in sight and hence, is [-intense]. This distinction is reflected in the semantically well-formed (26a) as opposed to the unacceptable (26b):

(26a)   I <u>watched (looked at)</u> it carefully!
(26b)   *I <u>saw</u> it carefully!

For this reason, there are situations wherein **watch** may occur with the progressive aspect but not **see**, as the progressive aspect is an event-highlighting aspect, and **seeing**, which is fortuitous in nature, is too casual an event to be highlighted. E.g.,

(27a)   I <u>watched</u> him talking to the salesman.
(27b)   I <u>saw</u> him talking to the salesman.

(28a)   I <u>was watching</u> him talking to the salesman when the boss came in.
(28b)   *I <u>was seeing</u> him talking to the salesman when the boss came in.

However,r there are cases when **see** does occur in the progressive. Let us examine such sentences with respect to the modes of materialization of the verbs.

(7b)   Oh, I'<u>m seeing</u> stars. Help me to a chair, quick!
(7c)   I'<u>ve been seeing</u> sunspots since yesterday.

(29)   Looking at the stock indices, he sighed, "I'm <u>seeing</u> my life savings going down the drain."

(30a)   <u>Am</u> I <u>seeing</u> a ghost?
(30b)   "<u>Am</u> I <u>seeing</u> my wife there?" asked the patient with one eye still in bandage.

In all the sentences above, the *seeing* is materialized with a high degree of concentration on the part of the agent. In sentence (30b), the person with poor eyesight was looking hard at the object he was trying to identify. In all the other sentences above, as well as Comrie's 'seeing pink elephants' in (7a), the agent was seeing something that can be generally characterized as 'spectacular'. When one sees something spectacular, he sees it hard, much harder than when he sees a tree or a lamppost by the road. This is the factor which makes the seeing compatible with the event-highlighting aspect, the progressive. This captured feature is again [intense].

Similar to the case of wait, watch, which requires concentration and is therefore usually [+intense] in modality, may appear with the perfect aspect to denote an on-going process when the time span is long enough. E.g.,

(27c)   I <u>have watched</u>, <u>watched</u>, and <u>watched</u>, but nothing has happened so far.

To sum up, **see** in its typical sense of visual perception (e. g. 27b) is [-intense] in modality and hence is incompatible with the event-highlighting progressive aspect. But when the object that has come in sight is more spectacular than ordinary, it immediately arrests the agent's attention and the seeing becomes an intense event. Thus, the verb becomes compatible with the progressive aspect.

Another case when seeing becomes [+intense] is when it is materialized with a purpose. E.g.,

(31)   Dr. Lee <u>is seeing</u> a patient now.
(32)   Mrs. Robinson <u>is seeing</u> a younger man.
(33)   We <u>have been seeing</u> a lot of houses lately.

4.3. Discussions on *keep/leave*.

It has been pointed out (Chen 1986:137, 150) that when a perfect continuous aspect is paired with a short time span as in the frame

F1:   X **has been V-ing** (NP) **for the last ten minutes,** we tend to expect something active or physical going on. Hence, sentence (35a), wherein the verbs are [-active], is unacceptable and (34), wherein the verbs are [+active], and (35b), wherein the time span is long enough, are well-formed:

(34) John <u>has been washing/painting</u> his car in the garage for the last ten minutes.

(35a) *John <u>has been keeping/leaving</u> his car in the garage <u>for the last ten minutes</u>. (He is now on his way to the airport for a vacation abroad.)

(35b) John <u>has been keeping/leaving</u> his car in the garage <u>for the last two weeks</u>.

However, given a deliberate context, sentence (35a) may become acceptable. For instance, in a competition where people have to sneak their cars into a garage and keep them there undetected for as long as possible, as in (35c):

(35c) John <u>has been keeping/leaving</u> his car in the garage for the last ten minutes, and still nobody knows about it.

The 'keeping one's car in the garage' in this special context of a competition exhibits a physical modality which is different from the ordinary 'keeping one's car in the garage' when it is not used, as in (35a). While the latter expresses an inactive and unattended situation, the former expresses a constructive continuum of a situation which is intensely dynamic.

This example illustrates the point that a [-active] verb, even one that contains no specific action, may acquire a modality that is similar to [+active] when it is materialized in a special way or context. This captured modality is again [intense].

5. The Genuine Non-dynamic States: the Chinese Stative Verbs.

In Chinese, words such as paioliang '(be) pretty, (be) good-looking, congming '(be) smart; (be) cleaver, pianyi '(be) inexpensive; (be) cheap', etc. are generally termed as adjectives by the grammarians and (stative) verbs by the linguists. Underlying this discrepancy is the dual function of these words; they have both the attributive and the predicative functions, which make them resemble both the adjectives and the verbs in languages like English. For instance, used attributively:

    (36a)   *piaoliang* xiaojie   'pretty girl(s)'

    (37a)   *congming* haizi   'smart kid(s)'

    (38a)   *pianyi* dongxi   'cheap item(s)'

And used as predicates:

    (36b)   Ta *piaoliang*, ni ye *paioliang*.
                  she-pretty, you-too-pretty.
                  She is pretty, and you are also pretty.

    (36c)   Ta *piaoliang* duo le.
                  she-pretty-much-(particle)
                  She is much prettier (than Mary/before), OR
                  She has become pretty/prettier.

    (37b)   Ta hen *congming*.
                  she-very-smart
                  She is very smart.

    (37c)   Ta zheci *congming* le.
                  she-this time-smart-(particle)
                  This time she is smart, OR
                  She has become smart/smarter this time.

    (38b)   Zhe dongxi zhen *pianyi*.
                  this-thing-really-cheap

This thing/item is really cheap.

(38c) Zhe dongxi xianzai *pianyi* le.
this-thing-now-cheap-(particle)
This thing/item is(/has become) cheap(er) now.

As shown in the above examples, these words have an attributive function, which makes them resemble the adjectives in English; they also have a predicative function, which makes them resemble the verbs in English. In the 'c' series of the examples, they occur before le, which has a dual identity of a particle indicating change of state and a verbal suffix indicating completion or perfection.

However, while other types of verbs may occur with the imperfective marker zai, e.g.,

(39) Ta zai *xiang/kan/guan*,
she-{zai}-thinking/looking/be in charge
She is thinking/looking/in charge,

this category of adjective-verb words cannot occur with the imperfective (or, progressive, in some analyses) marker zai:

(36/7d) *Ta zai *paioliang/congmin*.
She is becoming prettier/smarter.

(38d) *Zhe dongxi zai *pianyi*.
This thing is becoming cheaper.

Hence, it seems that these adjective-verb words in Chinese are the ones that denote genuinely non-dynamic situations. The English state verbs are still dynamic in their modality.

6. Summary and Conclusion.

Previous works categorized verbs into STATES and DYNAMIC

SITUATIONS by distinguishing two types of physical modalities: [-dynamic /active] and [+dynamic/active]. The present study, on the other hand, proposes a distinction between a [+dynamic, -active] modality and a [+dynamic, +active] modality. Here, [dynamic] is defined as POTENT or VIABLE; [active] is MOTIONAL, either physically or logically (e.g. *grow, change*, etc.) defined. Under the category of [-active] comes the division of [+intense] and [-intense], which are references to the modes of materialization in terms of potency, viability, effort, concentration, etc. of the physical or mental involvement on the part of the agent. Unlike [active] which is always an inherent and intrinsic feature, [intense] is a relative and gradient value and a variable. This is not a mere difference in terminology; it is a discovery of the true aspectual character of the English stative verbs, which both justifies their syntactic behaviors and account for the semantic characterizations.

The theoretical departure of the present analysis lies in the recognition that all English verbs are [+dynamic] in modality. This finding is deduced from two types of evidence: 1) Syntactically, all those verbs classified as states in previous works may occur in a progressive aspect, even though that may not be their typical usage. 2) Semantically, contrary to the definition ascribed by Comrie (1976:49), states may require energy or effort to continue; they may discontinue without anything happening to change them, they may be heterogeneous and changing throughout their duration.

While the claim that all English verbs are [+dynamic] in modality may appear to be a drastic departure from the previous treatments; it may turn out to be not at all surprising when the English verbal system is compared with that of Chinese. In Chinese, state verbs are often referred to as 'adjectives' by the laymen, school teachers, or even some grammarians. These Chinese 'adjectives' can function either as attributives or predicates (Chao 1968:663); they may occur with the perfective marker le, but may not occur with either the imperfective (or 'progressive' in some analyses) marker zai or the progressive marker -zhe. Perhaps, Chinese verbs of this type are the ones that are genuinely [-dynamic] in modality.

REFERENCES

CHAFE, Wallace L. 1970. *Meaning and the Structure of Language.* University of Chicago Press.

CHEN, Chung-yu. 1978. Aspectual features of the verb and the relative positions of the locative. *Journal of Chinese Linguistics* 6.1.76-103.

CHEN, Chung-yu. 1982. Time structure of English verbs. *Papers in Linguistics* 15.3.181-90.

CHEN, Chung-yu. 1986. On the physical Modality of English Verbs. *Papers in Linguistics* 19.2.131-54.

COMRIE, Bernard. 1976. *Aspect.* Cambridge University Press.

DOWTY, David R. 1977. Towards a semantic analysis of verb aspect and the English 'imperfective' progressive. *Linguistics and Philosophy* 1.45-77.

LYONS, John. 1977. *Semantics* (Vols 1 & 2). Cambridge University Press.

QUIRK, Randolph, Sideny GREENBAUM, Geoffrey LEECH and Jan SVARTVIK. 1972. *A Grammar of Contemporary English.* Longman, London.

VENDLER, Zeno. 1967. *Linguistics in Philosophy.* Cornell University Press.

INDEX 索引

A

acceptability test	可接受度之測驗	101-102
[-active] action verbs	[−動態]的動作動詞	20, 110-111, 114-115
active inceptive motion	動態的發端動作	15, 20, 27, 122-124
[+ → -active] verbs	[+ →− 動態] 動詞	20, 22, 27-29, 32, 71-73, 90, 115-116, 121-122, 125, 127

B

Ba constructions	把字句	30-31
backgrounding	後景	86-88
Body postures	身體姿態	20-21, 71-73, 90, 150

C

categorical notions	絕對概念	47-50, 108
causation (as in contrast to strong inception)	使動關系（與強式發端對比）	123
complement of extent	程度補語	43, 45
complement of result or extent	結果或程度補語	35, 50-51
context	情境	115

D

derived autonomy for inanimate subjects	無生命主語的衍生自主	23
deictic notions	指示概念	114

distant haplology	遠距離叠音刪簡	8-10, 12-13, 16, 31
disposal verbs	處置動詞	110, 113-114, 117
[durative]	持續性	107, 115-117
durative background	持續後景	63-65, 68, 89
[+dynamic, -active]	[+動性，-動態]	15
dynamic continuum of a [-active] state of affairs	[-動態]狀況裡的動性的持續	125-126, 158
dynamism in states	狀態裡的動性	152

E

external dynamic situation	外界的動性情況	65-67

F

foregrounding	前景	87-88
futurative progressives	表未來時式的進行態式	108, 113

H

haplology	叠音刪簡	8-10, 12-13, 16, 31

I

imperfective progressives	表事件未完成的進行態式	109-110, 113, 115-117
instantaneous transitions	瞬間轉變	108-110, 114
intensity in [-active] verbs	[-動態]動詞的強烈度	153-158
interrelationships	相關性	60-63, 83
iterative progressives	表重復的進行態式	108, 110, 116-117
interval transitions	緩慢轉變	114-115

L

lexical items	詞條	19, 112-123

M

manipulation verbs	操作動詞	113-114, 117
momentary actions	瞬間動作	108
'motional meaning' for verbs	動詞的動態語意	149
motional vs static	動態與靜態	150
mutation of aspectual characters	態式性向的突變	126-127

N

nominalizer de	名物化虛詞的	38, 42

O

one manifestation for two verbs	兩個動詞一個顯像	67-68, 88, 93
orientation or affiliation	取向或相屬	70-71

P

patient	受事（者）	67
perfective continuous	完成進行式	108, 114-117
perfective suffix -le	完成式后綴－了	15-16, 18, 21-22
physical modality (of verbs)	（動詞的）形體貌相	119-140
point transitions (=instantaneous transitions)	切點轉變（＝瞬間轉變）	109
potency and viability in [-active] verbs	[－動態]動詞的能力與活力	150-151, 153
potential particle de	表可能性的虛詞得	38, 40
pragmatic situations	現實、情況	83
predicative complement	述詞補語	35, 39, 43, 45, 52-56

predominant vs subordinate: of actions occurring simultaneously	主導與從屬：論同時發生的動作間的關係	63-65
process	歷程動詞	86, 114
progressives:	進行式：	
an event-highlighting aspect	突顯事件的態式	155-157
Dowty's analysis	Dowty的分析	113-115
futurative	表未來時式	108, 113
iterative	表重復	108, 110, 116-117

Q

qualification of an action	動作的定性	107, 112
quantification of an action	動作的計量	107, 111
quasi-active verbs	半動態動詞	26, 150

R

relative weighting	比重	63-65, 83-86
resultant static state of affairs	動作結果的靜態情景	21-23, 27-28

S

scalar notions	程度性概念	47-50, 108
semantic constraints	語意限制	79-83
selectional restrictions	選擇限制	16, 18
simple continuous aspect	簡單進行式	107-108
spontaneous effect	即時效力	69, 88, 93
states: no effort/energy?	狀態：不涉及力量或精力？	147-148
states: homogeneity?	狀態：一致性？	148-149
states: lastingness?	狀態：持續性？	148

static position (body postures)	靜態姿勢（身體姿態）	20-21, 71-73, 90, 150
'stative meaning' for verbs	動詞的靜態語意	149-150
strong inception	強勢發端	15, 20, 27, 122-124
subordinate readings vs corrdinate readings of clauses	子句間的從屬或對等關係的語意解釋	91-94
substitution drills	替換練習	103

T

time structure (of verbs)	（動詞的）時間結構	107-118
terminal aspect marker: Zero	終結態式記號：零	1, 15-16, 18, 21, 31
terminal cross-section of an action	動作的終結斷面	15, 19, 30
[+ → -transitive] transmutation	[+ →— 及物] 突變	29, 124-125, 127

V

V1-zhe... V2 structure:	V1-着...V2 結構	
V1, V2 interrelationship	V1, V2 相關性	60-63, 80-83
semantic constraints	語意限制	60-64
involving one active action only	只涉及一個動態動詞	65-73
V2-negation test for a coordinate reading	判斷并列結構的第二動詞否定測驗	92-93
Vendler's accomplishment terms	Vemdler 的'完成詞類'	111-112, 114
Vendler's achievement terms	Vendler 的'達成詞類'	108, 113
Vendler's concept of inception	Vendler 的'發端的概念'	119-120
Vendler's 'generic states'	Vendler 的'泛指性靜態'	107-108, 117-119, 150
Vendler's 'set terminus'	Vendler 的'預定的終結'	112
Vendler's state terms	Vendler 的'靜態詞類'	108
Venue-oriented verbs	場所相關動詞	19, 22, 27

verb-complement constructions	動補結構	36
verbs of inert perception	感官動詞	145, 150
verbs of unspecified and multi-formed realizations	不定型多樣體現動詞	114-115, 153-155
V-R compounds	動結複合詞	36, 38, 43

W

weak inception	弱勢發端	121

Y

yibian V1... yibian V2	一邊 V1...一邊 V2	62, 66, 73-76, 82, 84-85

Z

zai: aspect marker	在：動貌標誌	8, 11-12, 16, 18, 20, 22, 31
zai: preposition	在：介詞	20, 26, 31
-zhe as a progressive marker	着：進行態式的記號	11-12, 16, 18, 21-22

漢英語法・語意學論集（全一冊）

著 作 者：陳　　　重　　　瑜
出 版 者：臺 灣 學 生 書 局
本書局登
記證字號：行政院新聞局局版臺業字第一一〇〇號
發 行 人：丁　　　文　　　治
發 行 所：臺 灣 學 生 書 局
　　　　　臺北市和平東路一段一九八號
　　　　　郵政劃撥帳號00024668
　　　　　電話：3634156
　　　　　FAX：(02) 3636334
印 刷 所：常 新 印 刷 有 限 公 司
　　　　　地　址：板橋市翠華街8巷13號
　　　　　電　話：9524219・9531688
香港總經銷：藝 文 圖 書 公 司
　　　　　地址：九龍偉業街99號連順大厦五字
　　　　　樓及七字樓　電話：7959595

定價　精裝新台幣二二〇元
　　　平裝新台幣一六〇元

中華民國八十一年八月初版

80258　版權所有・翻印必究

ISBN 957-15-0406-8（精裝）
ISBN 957-15-0407-6（平裝）

MONOGRAPHS ON MODERN LINGUISTICS

Edited by

Ting-chi Tang

National Tsing Hua University

ASSOCIATE EDITORIAL BOARD

1. Jin-nan Lai (Tamkang University)
2. Yu-hwei E. Lü (National Taiwan Normal University)
3. Kuang Mei (National Taiwan University)
4. Chien Ching Mo (National Chengchi University)
5. Tsai-fa Cheng (University of Wisconsin)
6. Jeffrey C. Tung (National Taiwan Normal University)

現代語言學論叢編輯委員會

總編纂：湯廷池（國立清華大學）
編輯委員：施玉惠（國立師範大學）
　　　　　梅　　廣（國立臺灣大學）
　　　　　莫建清（國立政治大學）
　　　　　董昭輝（國立師範大學）
　　　　　鄭再發（美國威斯康辛大學）
　　　　　賴金男（私立淡江大學）

（以姓氏筆劃多寡為序）

現代語言學論叢書目

甲類① 湯廷池著：國語變形語法研究第一集：移位變形
② 鄭良偉
　　鄭謝淑娟著：臺灣福建話的語音結構及標音法
③ 湯廷池著：英語教學論集
④ 孫志文著：語文教學改革芻議
⑤ 湯廷池著：國語語法研究論集
⑥ 鄭良偉著：臺灣與國語字音對應規律的研究
⑦ 董昭輝著：從「現在完成式」談起
⑧ 鄧守信著：漢語及物性關係的語意研究
⑨ 溫知新
　　楊福綿編：中國語言學名詞滙編
⑩ 薛鳳生著：國語音系解析
⑪ 鄭良偉著：從國語看臺語的發音
⑫ 湯廷池著：漢語詞法句法論集
⑬ 湯廷池著：漢語詞法句法續集
⑭ 石毓智著：肯定和否定的對稱與不對稱

乙類① 鄧守信著：漢語主賓位的語意研究（英文本）
② 溫知新等十七人著：中國語言學會議論集（英文本）
③ 曹逢甫著：主題在國語中的功能研究（英文本）
④ 湯廷池等十八人著：1979年亞太地區語言教學研討會論集
⑤ 莫建清著：立陶宛語語法試論（英文本）
⑥ 鄭謝淑娟著：臺灣福建話形容詞的研究（英文本）
⑦ 曹逢甫等十四人著：第十四屆國際漢藏語言學會論文集（英文本）
⑧ 湯廷池等十人著：漢語句法、語意學論集（英文本）
⑨ 顧百里著：國語在臺灣之演變（英文本）

MONOGRAPHS ON MODERN LINGUISTICS

Edited by

Ting-chi Tang

National Tsing Hua University

ASSOCIATE EDITORIAL BOARD

1. Jin-nan Lai (Tamkang University)
2. Yu-hwei E. Lü (National Taiwan Normal University)
3. Kuang Mei (National Taiwan University)
4. Chien Ching Mo (National Chengchi University)
5. Tsai-fa Cheng (University of Wisconsin)
6. Jeffrey C. Tung (National Taiwan Normal University)

現代語言學論叢編輯委員會

總編纂：湯廷池（國立清華大學）
編輯委員：施玉惠（國立師範大學）
　　　　　梅　　廣（國立臺灣大學）
　　　　　莫建清（國立政治大學）
　　　　　董昭輝（國立師範大學）
　　　　　鄭再發（美國威斯康辛大學）
　　　　　賴金男（私立淡江大學）

（以姓氏筆劃多寡為序）

現代語言學論叢書目

甲類① 湯廷池著：國語變形語法研究第一集：移位變形
② 鄭良偉
　　鄭謝淑娟著：臺灣福建話的語音結構及標音法
③ 湯廷池著：英語教學論集
④ 孫志文著：語文教學改革芻議
⑤ 湯廷池著：國語語法研究論集
⑥ 鄭良偉著：臺灣與國語字音對應規律的研究
⑦ 董昭輝著：從「現在完成式」談起
⑧ 鄧守信著：漢語及物性關係的語意研究
⑨ 溫知新
　　楊福綿編：中國語言學名詞滙編
⑩ 薛鳳生著：國語音系解析
⑪ 鄭良偉著：從國語看臺語的發音
⑫ 湯廷池著：漢語詞法句法論集
⑬ 湯廷池著：漢語詞法句法續集
⑭ 石毓智著：肯定和否定的對稱與不對稱

乙類① 鄧守信著：漢語主賓位的語意研究(英文本)
② 溫知新等
　　十七人著：中國語言學會議論集(英文本)
③ 曹逢甫著：主題在國語中的功能研究(英文本)
④ 湯廷池等
　　十八人著：1979年亞太地區語言教學研討會論集
⑤ 莫建清著：立陶宛語語法試論(英文本)
⑥ 鄭謝淑娟著：臺灣福建話形容詞的研究(英文本)
⑦ 曹逢甫等
　　十四人著：第十四屆國際漢藏語言學會論文集(英文本)
⑧ 湯廷池等
　　十人著：漢語句法、語意學論集(英文本)
⑨ 顧百里著：國語在臺灣之演變(英文本)

⑩ 顧百里著：白話文歐化語法之研究（英文本）
⑪ 李梅都著：漢語的照應與刪簡（英文本）
⑫ 黃美金著：「態」之探究（英文本）
⑬ 坂本英子著：從華語看日本漢語的發音
⑭ 曹逢甫著：國語的句子與子句結構（英文本）
⑮ 陳重瑜著：漢英語法・語意學論集（英文本）

語文教學叢書書目

① 湯廷池著：語言學與語文教學
② 董昭輝著：漢英音節比較研究（英文本）
③ 方師鐸著：詳析「匆匆」的語法與修辭
④ 湯廷池著：英語語言分析入門：英語語法教學問答
⑤ 湯廷池著：英語語法修辭十二講
⑥ 董昭輝著：英語的「時間框框」
⑦ 湯廷池著：英語認知語法：結構、意義與功用（上集）
⑧ 湯廷池著：國中英語教學指引